21

G000109651

Wicked Hot

ALSO BY GENNITA LOW

Go to http://www.gennita-low.com/site/index.php for more information

BIG BAD WOLF

~ ~ Crossfire Series ~ ~
PROTECTOR
HUNTER
SLEEPER
HER SECRET PIRATE (short story)
WARRIOR

~ ~ Hot Spies Series ~ ~
DANGEROUSLY HOT
SIZZLE

~ ~ Secret Assassins (S.A.S.S.) ~ ~
INTO DANGER
FACING FEAR
TEMPTING TROUBLE

~.~.Super Soldier Spy ~ ~
VIRTUALLY HIS
VIRTUALLY HERS

~ ~Sex Lies & Spies~ ~
*novella series
THE GAME
THE PAWN
THE SEAL

~ ~Susan Stoker's Special Forces (Kindle World)
NO PROTECTION

~ ~Cristin Harber's TITAN World~ ~
THE EDGE OF TEMPTATION

Wicked Hot

By Gennita Low

A MacKenzie Family Novella

Introduction by Liliana Hart

EVIL EYE
CONCEPTS

Wicked Hot
A MacKenzie Family Novella
Copyright 2017 Gennita Low
ISBN: 978-1-942299-88-2

Introduction copyright 2017 Liliana Hart

Published by Evil Eye Concepts, Incorporated

All rights reserved. No part of this book may be reproduced, scanned, or distributed in any printed or electronic form without permission. Please do not participate in or encourage piracy of copyrighted materials in violation of the author's rights.

This is a work of fiction. Names, places, characters and incidents are the product of the author's imagination and are fictitious. Any resemblance to actual persons, living or dead, events or establishments is solely coincidental.

ACKNOWLEDGMENTS

Many thanks to Liliana Hart for inviting me to write in her MacKenzie series. It was exciting mashing her world with mine. It was an honor to be part of her team.

Thank you always to Ranger Buddy. His strength supports mine.

AN INTRODUCTION TO THE MACKENZIE FAMILY WORLD

Dear Readers,

I'm thrilled to announce the MacKenzie Family World is returning! I asked five of my favorite authors to create their own characters and put them into the world you all know and love. These amazing authors revisited Surrender, Montana, and through their imagination you'll get to meet new characters, while reuniting with some of your favorites.

These stories are hot, hot, hot and packed with action and adventure—exactly what you'd expect from a MacKenzie story. It was pure pleasure for me to read each and every one of them and see my world through someone else's eyes. They definitely did the series justice, and I hope you discover five new authors to put on your auto-buy list.

Make sure you check out Spies and Stilettos, a brand new, full-length MacKenzie novel written by me. This will be the final installment of the MacKenzie series, featuring Brady Scott and Elena Nayal. After eighteen books of my own and ten books written by other bestselling authors in the MacKenzie World, it's going to be difficult to say goodbye to a family I know as well as my own. Thank you for falling in love with the MacKenzies.

So grab a glass of wine, pour a bubble bath, and prepare to Surrender.

Love Always,
Liliana Hart

* * * *

Available now!

Spies & Stilettos by Liliana Hart
Trouble Maker by Liliana Hart
Rush by Robin Covington

Never Surrender by Kaylea Cross
Avenged by Jay Crownover
Bullet Proof by Avery Flynn
Delta: Rescue by Cristin Harber
Hot Witness by Lynn Raye Harris
Deep Trouble by Kimberly Kincaid
Wicked Hot by Gennita Low
Desire & Ice by Christopher Rice

CHAPTER ONE

Kirk's phone was on silent and it'd been vibrating for the last few minutes. He didn't want to walk away just yet.

Mary MacKenzie was being laid to rest on a rainy day. There were so many Navy SEALs and military personnel gathered, one would think a very important warrior had passed. But this was Mary MacKenzie, mother to the MacKenzie brothers, a sweet woman who had managed to get so many warriors who came to visit the MacKenzie compound to love her as they would their own mother. And under the cloudy sky, rain coming down, these brave men had tears in their eyes.

Kirk Ryan had attended more funerals than he'd like. He came from a military background, with an extended family of friends, relatives, and associates who interconnected in various government branches or, like him, in independent contract service, as his kind sometimes referred to itself when talking to strangers. Attending funerals was important to an NSA fixer like him. People who were hard to get ahold of, whose security was so tight one would have to go through layers of red tape to reach, were suddenly standing within talking distance. He usually could get an introduction or a chance to get someone's attention.

He was a troubleshooter, one who could find a solution to a difficult situation, but today, he could not fix this. He could not be objective when two dozen SEALs, some of whom were his good friends, men with lethal eyes and steady hands when it came to warfare, openly cried in the rain at the words softly spoken. A beautiful celebration of a life. His cousin, Archer, standing beside him, was all choked up for a few moments.

He touched Archer's elbow and signaled he had to go. Depending on his contact, he was going to miss his turn to offer the MacKenzies his condolences. His cousin nodded back at him.

Kirk hung back as the people moved forward to file past the grieving family, looking for the right opening to melt away from the crowd. He was good at disappearing without people noticing. As he took a few steps backward, his gaze caught Declan MacKenzie's.

Declan wasn't most people, though. He ran MacKenzie Securities and before that, black ops for the government. A few friends had joked with him that Declan had eyes on the back of his head because he always seemed to know everything happening around him. Just a glance and the message was conveyed.

Kirk paused for a moment, wondering why he was being told to stay put. It had to be something important for Declan to single him out. He nodded back before sidling off to find a private spot to make his phone call.

"Indonesia," the voice on the other end said. "Takeoff at 0600 DC Wednesday."

His next stop. Instructions arrived via an encrypted message. Usually, he was given three days to prepare but this time, it was less than forty-eight hours. Something urgent. He resisted the urge to leave.

Usually, he would excuse himself as soon as possible to find out more information about his next assignment. Prep work was important in his job. However, paying his final respects was important too and although he was a loner by nature, this was family. His heart ached with the loss of Mary MacKenzie. Even though he hadn't hung around her as much as some of his friends and cousins, she had always remembered to send him cards and invitations to family get-togethers and always was so sweet and kind when he did manage to show up. No one could resist her gentle charm. It was going to be so hard to come visit and not see her familiar figure. It'd be a hundred times more so for the MacKenzie brothers, who had adored their beloved mother.

He sighed and bowed his head, wishing he could do more than give his friends words of comfort.

Later in the evening

"Thank you for staying," Declan said, looking around the room. "I know some of you are keeping a tight schedule. I appreciate that you've made time to be here."

Kirk studied the group sitting in the private room—mostly SEALs, the MacKenzie brothers, and several of the operatives working for Declan. He was a little surprised. He hadn't expected to be included in such an exclusive group meeting.

It'd been a very long day emotionally and the mood in the room was subdued. Some of the men had changed out of their suits and ties and some of the SEALs were already back in fatigues, with their gear at their feet. Even so, there was a quiet air of expectancy. Declan had summoned them here for a reason.

"Coffee, anyone?" One of the operatives showed a pot.

"Yeah."

"Please."

"Wish there was something stronger," one of the SEALs said. "Sorry, Dec. Didn't mean to be disrespectful. I just heard all the details two days ago. About Holland. About what he did. It's finally sinking in."

Declan's expression hardened. He nodded. "I know, Lucas. Holland's betrayal has really shaken the Teams. Those who couldn't make it here, who knew Mom, called or sent messages. But mostly, I'm getting asked whether it's true, that one of our own would be responsible for her…" He paused, swallowed, and continued, "death. But this is why I've asked the STAR Team to be present at this meeting."

"What can we do to help?" Another of the team spoke up.

"I've talked to Admiral Madison, Hawk, and hope to borrow a few of you for a mission," Declan said.

Kirk looked closely at the team of SEALs sitting next to Lucas, mentally recalling their names from earlier introductions. Hawk was obviously the leader and next to him were Jazz, Mink, and Milos. The other three were scattered around the room. He'd heard about this team. STAR—Standing and Ready—SEALs, a special team under the command of Admiral Madison. Off the books, all black ops, connected to certain joint ventures to look for CIA moles abroad.

Lucas was a big guy. His tight grip on his soda can betrayed his anger. Kirk understood. The SEAL teams were very close knit, sort of a "one-for-all-and-all-for-one" mentality. When one of their own was the traitor, everyone was affected. Kirk's job as a fixer gave him a greyer world view. His was a shadowy existence, filled with double agents and non-aligned contractors, people who gave allegiance to different factions for personal gain. Life wasn't a solid brotherhood.

"Why isn't my old team here too? Only Brady is present," Shane MacKenzie demanded, his voice hoarser than usual. "Why is Kirk here and none of our top operatives?"

Kirk had wondered about that too. These men weren't the usual MacKenzie contractors. Also, getting Admiral Madison's team for any operation was a big deal.

Shane was the commander of the Silver Team at NEVGRU but had recently been forced to retire because of a missile hit that had cost him a leg. Kirk knew, from his cousin, how difficult a time he'd had with adjusting to life, that it was almost touch-and-go for a while. Looking at him right now, one would never know, though. Shane was wearing a prosthetic leg and had been standing at attention all day. Handsome devil. Still fit as an active SEAL, apparently, since he was the one who had taken down Holland. All day, Kirk had studied him, wondering at a quiet side of Shane he'd never seen before and at the woman—he'd heard that was his current love interest—at his side. Right now, because of the subject matter, he had the look of a military man about to draw blood.

"We only need one team," Dec replied. "Brady and his team have to return to base and take care of their other assignments. Admiral Madison has generously offered to help out with this operation. Kirk's here because his next assignment is tied to what I want—finding the bastards behind Holland."

Kirk set his cup down. Finally. He'd been patiently waiting. "Indonesia?" he asked. No need to give any details. "I thought you killed Petrovich."

"Lacey did," Shane affirmed, his voice grim.

Kirk blinked. Lacey? As in Shane's girlfriend, the woman who had been by his side most of the day, Lacey? That revelation was new. He turned to Dec. "Petrovich's involvement signaled Russian infiltration," he said. "Why would my going to Indonesia be connected to you? And the STAR team?"

"Because you're heading to the Interpol gathering in Bali."

Kirk's eyebrows shot up. "You seem to know more about my next job than I do."

Declan nodded brusquely. "Knowing what's going on in the world is my job. This time, it's personal. At this moment, there are twelve hundred member delegations from over a hundred countries heading there to this assembly on a private island near Bali, many of whom are unaware of a sudden threat hanging over their heads. Your job is to negotiate the release of three Americans—two scientists and one operative—before the militant kidnappers shoot a missile toward that island. I want in on this operation. One of those scientists and the operative are my people. Under questioning, Holland has confirmed enough details to prove Petrovich was behind their disappearance and that the militants were going to give them to him in exchange for a large sum of money. Unfortunately, Petrovich is dead. This is their Plan B."

"Wait, Dec. Why are you not sending our men in? Sorry, Hawk, but this should be Brady or me running the operation," Shane interrupted.

Declan turned and gave his brother a level look. "Because Holland also revealed Petrovich had several SEALs in his pocket and that there were other rogue operatives who had lured those three men currently held hostage. I can't chance sending any of our usual right now. It has to be Admiral Madison's team and some outside contractors so none of those bastards are warned. Your job is here, Shane. You have to hand-pick a few trusted men and discover who else had been in Petrovich's pocket. Kirk, those scientists were taken because of new bio-inventions wanted by many governments, so the stakes are high."

"Fuck." Lucas's muttered curse came out succinctly in the pause that followed Declan's bombshell as everyone digested the revelation.

Kirk understood the shocked silence. One SEAL traitor was a tremor among the brotherhood. A group? Taking out their own? It was an earthquake. As a troubleshooter, he quickly thought about everything that he needed to get together before the next move.

"There are several problems," he said. "Indonesia has seventeen thousand islands and to get information fast, I'm going to need to find a translator. If it's a group of rogue operatives who know you, they might not recognize me. But me and one of your translators? That's upping the chances. Also, you're going to have to go through red tape to talk to the high-level person who has contracted me for this negotiation deal. I can't just give you your scientist and man back without any explanation."

If he got them back alive. Depending on the factions, Indonesian militants were known to kill off their prisoners, even after the other party had paid ransom. The urgency of this mission lay in the imminent danger to twelve hundred people on an island. Ordinarily, his primary priority would be to stop the missile and then focus on the safe return of the three kidnapped victims. The two were tied together, but in the government's eyes, the Interpol international meeting would be the more important objective.

But this was now personal. His usual SOP wasn't going to be enough.

"Don't worry. No red tape. I have already made contact to meet with that person," Dec said.

Kirk's brows shot up. "I don't even know who's giving the orders."

Dec's reply was soft. "I do."

Of course Dec would know. He always knew. "What if that person refused to discharge the two back to you?" There must be a reason the two scientists had been together, after all. "I haven't read all my instructions and can't formulate a plan until I do—who's meeting me there, how to integrate Hawk's team in, the translator, operations personnel in Indonesia."

Dec shook his head. "Right now, just do as you normally do until I call after my meeting. McNeil usually is fast when it comes to decisions."

"Wait. McNeil, as in Jed McNeil?" Hawk interrupted.

"Yes," Dec confirmed.

The SEALs exchanged glances.

"We've been doing joint ventures with his commandos to retrieve missing CIA weapons stolen by CIA moles," Jazz said.

"Russian moles," Hawk added grimly.

Ah. The picture was getting clearer to him. "Petrovich is part of the group who has infiltrated the government," Kirk said. "Since the Gorman scandal, retrieving certain missing weapons is top priority."

Declan nodded grimly. "And the enemy has been trying to stop the bleeding. They've been trying to figure out which agency was going after them so efficiently. Petrovich was sent to neutralize the MacKenzies because we work closely with the government."

"But it's been Jed's outfit," Hawk said. "If anyone could get rules bent, it's Jed and his men. I've seen them in action."

Kirk scratched off the top line on his note pad. "Translator," he said.

"I have contact with someone who's holidaying there," Jade chimed in.

Jade worked for Declan. She was beautiful and lethal. One didn't mess around with her.

"She owes me a favor," Jade continued, "and will do it, no problem."

"Experience?" Kirk asked. He didn't want any by-the-book translator.

"She's a contract agent. GEM," she told him.

His expression must have betrayed him because in spite of the gravity of the situation, several of the SEALs snickered. GEM operatives were not his favorite people at the moment. His last run-in with one of them had ended with him naked and handcuffed to a bed, but that was another story he preferred not to share.

"She's good," Jade said. "She'll get things done."

"It'd better not be T," Hawk murmured. "She'd tie him up in strings."

"And eat him for a snack," someone else added.

"They all would," Jazz agreed, a slight smile forming before adding, "except Vivi, of course."

"He'd know," Lucas said, pointing a thumb at Jazz. "He's married to one of them and his Vivi had him for every meal. I was there. Saw the whole thing."

There were more snickers from the other guys.

Jade frowned. "Hey, don't mouth off on my friends. It isn't T. Her name's Surya. I'll call her after this meeting and set you two up. Details in an hour."

Kirk gave a mental sigh. "All right." GEM operative. It'd have to do.

"But McNeil first," Declan said. "Everyone keeps their satellite phone ready and the secured app uploaded for video feeds."

"Affirmative."

Declan exhaled. "Again, thank you for coming here on such short notice. Now, my brothers and I have to go back in and be with our father. Kirk, my helicopter will get you to your next stop. No traffic." He cricked his neck and then straightened before walking toward Kirk. "This is important to me."

Kirk shook his hand. "To me too, Dec. I'll do my best. Good luck with McNeil."

The corners of Dec's lips lifted. "It's all about what the other side wants. You should know that, as a negotiator."

Kirk nodded. The question was, what would the government's premier assassin want that Dec could offer? Jed McNeil, from what he knew, was an enigma. Like him, McNeil moved in the world of shadows, and even there, very few knew about him and the commandos under him, except they were all part of a government experiment. Kirk would give anything to be there at this meeting. The things he would learn. Instead, he got one GEM operative named Surya.

An Interpol convention.

Three kidnapped VIPs.

A missile in the hands of militants.

Jungles everywhere.

A GEM operative who, from his previous experience with them, probably would have her own agenda.

Oh yeah, what could go wrong?

* * * *

Declan wasn't in the mood for games. McNeil's reputation was solid but he tended to amuse himself with odd diversions as a way to probe his opponent's state of mind. An assassin must find ways to engage, he supposed.

He studied the man lounging against a picnic table by the basketball court. Dressed in a denim jacket and worn jeans and bouncing a ball, he looked like a walking advertisement for Active Guy. But Declan had been trained to look for the stuff that wasn't obvious. Like a certain stillness in the way the other man moved, no matter how casual he appeared. Like the extended boot, which he knew held a weapon. Like the choice of a playground as a meeting place. Damn it. McNeil *was* playing games.

He strode toward the figure. McNeil didn't turn around.

"Jed," Declan said.

"Dec."

McNeil finally straightened up and turned to face him, ball still in his hands. His light eyes, a strange silvery grey that had earned him the nickname "Ice" during their Ranger days,as always in the past, caught Dec's attention.

Declan returned the level gaze, studying the other man closely. He appeared the same. Closed up. Expressionless. He remembered the earlier years when that face was unguarded, especially when he talked about traveling and seeing the world, but as the years went by, with all the training, he'd become more remote every time they'd crossed paths.

With someone like Jed McNeil, one had to always be on one's toes. There were two choices whenever he dealt with the assassin.

Attack or be pursued. He chose the former.

"It's been—what—five or six years?" Dec said. "You disappeared from COMCEN and then word was, you reappeared after a year. What, were you afraid they'd replace you with a new Supersoldier Spy?"

He kept his voice lightly mocking. Back in the day, McNeil had been in a program called VIRUS, also privately dubbed Supersoldier Spy. However, there was a new game in town and Declan was privy to the fact that someone else was now being trained with that ridiculous title. He had an idea who the trainer was, but that information was top, top FYEO secret only a few people could confirm under threat of death. He watched with interest the slight lift of the corners of McNeil's mouth.

"You're just sore external contractors weren't allowed to compete for a chance to get the program," Jed said in his soft tone, the slight Irish lilt in his voice, signaling his relaxed state. If an assassin was ever relaxed, that was. Sometimes, when they'd met in the middle of an operation, Jed would speak to him in a different accent or not at all, remaining in character even in private.

Back to the so-called "program." All the government agencies had sent in one or two top operatives to be vigorously trained and to compete against one another. The winning agency received all the funding for the Supersoldier Spy Program. Declan had been intrigued with the addendum that the operative had to have "alternate mental" skills, besides that of soldiering and spying, as the FYEO papers he had viewed had called it. "Alternate skills" must involve something called the ability to enter "remote-viewing state."

That had stopped him in his tracks. Remote viewing? Didn't that run out of style with the government since those other weirdo secret projects like alien DNA testing and hallucinatory drugging of soldiers? But millions of dollars of funding was the reward and the cynical part of him knew certain agencies just wanted to win so they could allocate the money somewhere else in their own various programs. But from what he'd heard, there was definitely a candidate who had gone beyond expectations during the training and competition stages.

"True," he acknowledged, "but I'm surprised. What would you do with a remote viewing skill in virtual reality, McNeil? And why would your scientist be talking with mine about anything virtual?"

There it was. A narrowing of the eyes. It was a stab in the dark and he'd drawn a little blood. It was just a guess. His contacts had told him of the extensive virtual reality toys being created and experimented with at DARPA for COMCEN.

McNeil bounced the ball once. Twice. "A special exoskeleton suit is a nice weapon to own, isn't it? I'd imagine a securities firm with government connections and private funding for science projects would attract many enemy eyes sooner or later. Imagine my supersoldier spy and your version of the exoskeleton." His silver eyes challenged Declan to deny it. His voice hardened slightly. "Imagine our secrets in the hands of the enemies."

Declan schooled his expression. So, they too had been working on creating a special exoskeleton. Not a surprise. Everyone copied everyone in their race for science. And weaponry too. However, his hospital and its location was top secret and now he knew Jed McNeil knew about this. Damn sonofabitch always cut a little deeper.

"But you asked to see me, my friend," McNeil continued. "I'm all ears." He threw the ball at him, adding. "Make a hoop, get a point. Isn't that how we always play this game?"

CHAPTER TWO

Kirk received the call from Declan as soon as he got off the plane. The Bali Ngurah Rai International Airport was crowded.

"You're cutting it close," he said, inserting his earpiece. "I'd thought you would call sooner so I could chart some strategy here."

Being a fixer was all about the strategy, especially in something that involved hostage negotiation. He had already read up on all the files included in his assignment folio, but this wasn't an ordinary negotiation and extraction. He had traitor operatives who could jeopardize the whole deal.

"I had to finalize a few things after my meeting with McNeil," Declan said. "Also, Dad wanted a family meeting about wills and personal stuff. Mom left something for you, he said. A book you've been hunting for. So you'd better get this done ASAP."

Kirk almost stumbled in surprise. He swallowed. That sweet woman was just incredible. "I...don't know what to say." He finally got the words out. "I'm sorry, Dec. I can't think about that right now. I'm going to need to concentrate on making sure I get those bastards who were part of this."

"Yes." Dec's voice was gruff. "I wanted to tell you before we continue. Didn't want that to be the last piece of information, you know? You're family, Kirk."

Kirk picked up his carry-on and stepped on the escalator. "I know." He cleared his throat. He couldn't afford to feel any sorrow right now. Anger. That was a good emotion for revenge. Changing the subject, he said, "Security is tight here. Too many VIPs coming and going. Dec, is McNeil in or out? I need to know who the players are to make sure whose side everyone's on. I've studied the files and know the operatives who have done work for MacKenzie Securities before and shouldn't be here. If I see them—"

"Yes. If you see them, I did not send them. McNeil's agreed to help but I still need to coordinate certain details with him, with Hawk and his team, and with Shane. I've had to talk down Brady's arguments. Let's just say I have my hands full because everyone wants to do your job."

"Yes, I'm sure the NSA would love to hear about a bunch of SEALs in an unsanctioned extraction showing up with enough firepower to alarm a nation hosting an important Interpol meeting," Kirk said wryly. He could just imagine the international hullabaloo that would cause. "Tell me about McNeil. I've heard he's a tough devil. How did you get him to see things your way? Did you sell your soul?"

Dec gave a short bark of amusement. "Thanks for that laugh. Much needed." His sigh came through over the phone. "According to him, there's a nest of traitors out there. He's been chipping away for five years. Five fucking years, Kirk. I'm not going to let that happen. This isn't just about national security. This is about getting my mother's killers. That's the main thing. McNeil understands where I'm coming from and even offered his services. Besides, his inside connections with foreign governments allow him certain freedoms. He can move in and out without interference. I can't be there nor can any of my brothers or people, so I accepted."

He sounded tired. Kirk wondered when was the last time Dec slept. "Hey," he said, understanding the other man's need to be with family and also run an international operation. "You know I got this. You should be spending time with the family. It'll take at least another twelve to twenty-four hours of laying out the groundwork. As soon as I get the call from NSA that the kidnappers have contacted them again, you'll be the first to know, I promise."

"Right." Dec's tone of voice returned to business-like.

"Everything is ready. Your name has been added to the hotel guest list. It's full and security is tight everywhere. The GEM operative, Surya, is waiting for you in her suite, so that would save the need to meet in public. She has agreed to be a translator if there are any language problems. Remember, she's on vacation, or was, so you'll have to act as a good friend joining her. Be casual and bring some flowers, she said, because you're coming to celebrate her birthday and she's told the hotel front desk she was going to go sightseeing with you. That would be a good cover for both of you traveling around. I've read her file and she seems very capable. I've never had the need to use them for my ops before so you'll have to play it by ear. Jade assured me they are top-notch at what they do."

"Okay." Playing it by ear. He wasn't sure whether that was a good thing when it came to a GEM operative, but he didn't say anything for now. "I'll call as soon as I have everything lined up."

"Good luck."

After going through Customs and a visit to the bathroom, he was met by a driver holding up a sheet of cardboard with his name on it. He greeted the man and made a beeline to a flower stand to pick up a bouquet. Outside, the humidity hit him like a heavy slap of hot towels. It was like breathing in water.

Kirk studied the bustle of airport traffic, taking a few moments to adjust. He felt a trickle of perspiration running down his neck. He was going to need lots of refreshment today. And lighter clothes.

The drive to the hotel was mind-boggling, to say the least. He'd planned to read up on files and do some quick research on the GEM operative during the drive, but that flew out the window the moment they hit the main roads. Everyone appeared to think they had the right-of-way, with helmetless drivers on scooters zipping alongside cars and across lanes in front of oncoming traffic. Several times he had to stop himself from shouting out to the driver, who seemed unperturbed by the near-accidents. Instead, he just gripped his briefcase handle a little tighter and concentrated on not gritting his teeth.

The driver turned around at one point and said, in broken English, "You relaxed, ya? I take care of drive, no problem. Sit back and relax, ya? Be at hotel quick, quick, quick!"

Sit back and relax! Kirk pointed frantically at the windshield. "Bicyclist!" was all he could get out as he watched a young couple, the woman perched on the handle bars of a bicycle, merrily cross the intersection.

His driver wasn't even fazed by the near-miss. To Kirk's relief, he did return his attention to the road. "Don't worry, Sir. I drive faster so you get to hotel."

That didn't sound comforting at all. On the other hand, getting to the hotel faster might be good.

Kirk leaned back against the seat. He didn't need refreshments. He would need a whole bottle of whiskey after this ride. He made a mental note to make sure they hired a driver. There was no way he could ever drive around this area and not hit something.

By the time they reached the hotel, he felt even more tired than the usual jet lag-induced malaise. His check-in went smoothly, thank goodness, and within minutes, he was on the way to what he hoped was a quick introduction with Surya Tangers and then excuse himself so he could take a nice shower.

The suite was on the highest floor. There was a fantastic view when he emerged from the elevator. If he were the woman, he'd be annoyed at having his nice vacation interrupted by an assignment. He looked down at the flowers in his hand. They looked slightly wilted. He should just chuck them in the waste bin since they'd already done the job of giving the desired impression to the staff in the lobby. The clerk had given Kirk a knowing smile as he accepted his tip. The bellboy had offered to help take care of his carry-on so he could "quickly go up to the room to meet his lady friend." He'd declined the offer, of course, and just tipped the man.

Quickly there. Quickly up. Quickly done. That appeared to be the mode around here. As a fixer, he preferred thoroughness over speed. The way to get things done right was in the details.

Using his key card, he opened the double door to the suite. He stepped in and surveyed the whole place. *Jaysus.* It was like entering a secret doorway to a mansion. It looked like one of those movie star houses featured in magazines. Marble floor living area. Lush silk brocade curtains. Gold couches with mahogany tables. Deep carpeting leading to other smaller areas. Even a damn baby grand piano. Girl was serious about her vacation.

A sumptuous meal was set up on the dining table, the delicious scent of local spices tickling his nose, reminding him he hadn't eaten. His attention followed the soft music coming from one of the rooms. He turned toward it, wondering if he should announce himself. Maybe she didn't know he was here. That couldn't be. He was sure someone had already informed her of his arrival.

"Come on in," a voice called out from the room with the music. "I'm just getting your room ready."

Kirk walked into "his" room, flowers in one hand, pulling the briefcase on top of his carry-on with the other. The rollers hardly made a sound over the thick, soft cream carpet.

"I've set up a private link and checked to see if the wireless—" The woman turned to face him. "Oh!"

"You!"

Kirk dropped the flowers and luggage and lunged at his "girlfriend."

* * * *

Surya stood frozen for exactly one second. That one second cost her. Instead of running to the right and locking herself in the bathroom, she found that path cut off as a tall and muscular male body blocked her escape.

She should've guessed. Jade asking the favor had thrown her off from guessing it might be somebody she knew.

This vacation was so not. So, so not. It had started out great, until that phone call.

She should have booked a cruise.

She could have gone on that stupid camping trip with Marlena and Steve and played third wheel. On second thought, no. Anything but playing third wheel to Marlena and Steve.

"I really don't want to hurt you," she warned the angry, stalking male coming at her.

"I really want to hurt you. Maybe even kill you—after," he told her, "a spanking."

Sheesh. Men were so unforgiving when it came to their pride. She shrieked when he started to undo his belt.

"Oh, come on!" she said, backing a few steps. "My belt was much, much thinner than yours. And it was all done in fun."

"Uh-huh. You can explain to me later. Right now—"

He dove.

Surya ducked to the right.

While on the carpeted floor, he swung out a hand and caught hold of her leg. She twisted, trying to pull free and losing her balance. She fell onto the side of the bed. He came up on his knees and attempted to pull her around onto her front. She resisted, scooting further back on the bed. He followed, his hands grasping her thighs firmly.

Surya turned, picked up the nearest weapon, and bashed a pillow down onto his head. Sure, she was going to beat the man to death with a pretty silk pillow. A karate chop would do the job but that would mean hurting the man she'd told her friend she would protect. Also, she really, really liked this man a lot, even though the last time, they'd met under false pretenses. Okay, more than really, really liked. She clobbered his head with the pillow with renewed gusto.

Her unexpected visitor reached up and held onto the underside of her weapon. She tugged at it.

"Seriously? A pillow?" That familiar deep male voice that had whispered sweet nothings in her ear growled in disbelief. "If that's your weapon of choice, you aren't trying very hard to escape."

Surya peered over the silk pillow. "You're always overreacting. I'm trying to calm you down."

"Overre—I'm the calmest person I know!"

"You're shouting," she pointed out calmly.

He pushed the pillow up against her chest and effectively tackled her onto her back. She looked up at him. Rumpled dirty blond hair, angry blue eyes, lips she still dreamed about—she sighed loudly.

"Now you're manhandling your assistant," she said and watched those blue eyes get all fired up. She really did enjoy riling the man. He exuded this strange combination of nerdy and sexy strength that she found irresistible. "Is your name really Kirk? I prefer the other one. Anthony is so much more you."

"That's my middle name. Is Surya your real name?" he countered. He cocked his head. "It's got to be real, since Jade said you're a good friend. She wouldn't just make up a name…would she?"

Surya considered lying. She had lied the last time because she was on assignment. She'd regretted doing it, although she wasn't sure why. She lied to targets all the time. But he really wasn't a target; he was just someone who got in the way.

"I'm really Surya," she admitted.

"You left me tied up. You took something that belonged to me."

Surya bit down on her lip to keep from smiling. Actually, she'd left him tied up, naked. She'd also spanked his cute bottom a couple of times before she left, which was the reason he was still so pissed off, but it was better she left those details out for now.

"I took two things, actually, Kirk." She savored his name, testing. Okay, maybe he was all right as a Kirk. Kirk Anthony. How sexy was that?

He frowned and leaned closer. "You took the papers. What. Else?"

She winked. "Not going to tell you."

He was so close now she could lift her head and bite his chin. He smelled just the way she remembered, a masculine, woodsy scent, with a hint of vanilla, which went straight to her senses. Damn, why did the man smell so good? She sniffed appreciatively.

His frown deepened. "I don't stink that bad," he said, "so you can quit pretending. I can't think of what you could have stolen besides my papers." He paused, his eyes searching hers, then he said her name softly and slowly. "Surya."

The tone in his voice made her shiver. She'd always liked his voice, a deep, velvety timbre. She could sit enthralled, listening to him read the phone book. And that was one of the reasons she'd hightailed out of there six months ago. This man was dangerous to her.

"Surya," he repeated.

"That *is* my name…Kirk," she said. "I did try to find you, you know, but your fake identity made it difficult to discern which address to send the papers back to."

That jerked him back up. "Send the papers… You mean you were going to mail them back? Are you fucking insane? Those papers were worth a fortune!"

"You don't have to go all postal on me," she said, remembering now she'd wanted to see the look on his face when he received the item in the mail. She added in her best bored voice, "I'd have made sure the package was properly insured."

"Properly…" He groaned, then shook his head. "I need to go somewhere and think this through."

"You need to let me go so we can get to work," she pointed out.

"I need to put a hole in my head to work with you again," he gritted back.

She grinned up at the exasperated expression inches from her own. "How about a kiss first? I really, really prefer you giving me a kiss than putting a hole in your head and messing up those pretty lips."

His blue eyes became laser intense and she felt that tingly feeling again. Her heartbeat, which had slowed down during their conversation, sped back up.

"A kiss?" he rumbled. "I've been looking for you for six months and you expect a kiss?"

He'd been looking for her? Her toes curled.

"It's not like you didn't know where to look," she told him. "You knew I was with GEM."

"Since I couldn't give them your real ID, your handlers were clearly a bit more protective. But never mind. I got you now."

And he kissed her.

* * * *

Kirk knew he shouldn't have kissed her. The woman was bad news. One night with her six months ago had cost him major headaches with an assignment. Worse, he was angry for weeks because he'd thought—

No. The trouble had been he hadn't been thinking. His dick was. Every time "Salome" was nearby, all he'd wanted to do was spend time with her. She'd been upfront and told him she was a GEM agent, translating the documents to make sure they were the real thing. Her story had checked out. He hadn't known the real Salome Winger was tall, blonde, and forty-five years old.

Kissing her. He wanted to do more than that.

She tasted so damn familiar. A hint of mint. The sweet taste of warm woman. The promise of slow sex. He'd looked for her and promised himself that the next vacation he took, he would go after her and make her sorry she'd handcuffed him to the bed and left him. The memory of that made him lean down and kiss her harder. Her response was just as fierce and he felt her hands in his hair, pulling his head down even more.

He broke off the kiss and lay his forehead on hers. His breathing was ragged.

"Minx. I have no time for this. I have to freshen up and we need to get to work."

"Am I forgiven then?"

He lifted his head and glared down at that gorgeous, passionate face. "Of course not. Retribution will come later," he promised.

Her answering smile was wicked, and he wanted to kiss her some more. Giving her another dark look, he shifted his weight, freeing her. He sat up on the bed, regretting that work must come first. His cock was feeling more than regretful. She looked absolutely sinful, lying there on "his" bed, bare arms and legs, her skirt pulled up to show a hint of hot pink panties. Her dark hair, which had been knotted up, had come undone, the thick waves fanning out against the white sheets. Her dark eyes were slumberous and inviting, daring him. He shook his head. She was driving him crazy and it'd only been fifteen minutes since he'd laid eyes on her again.

He stood up. "Do I have to lock you out of my room so you won't steal any more of my stuff?" he asked, looking down at her.

She sniffed. "A girl borrows something and gets this horrible reputation." She stretched. "This bed is more comfy than mine."

Oh, she was good. Always trying to distract him. "Nope, not falling for that again," he said, and went to his dropped luggage.

"What are you doing?" she asked, propping her head up, watching him with narrowed eyes.

"Taking my stuff with me to the bathroom," he told her. "I believe you got us some food. Why don't I meet you there, across the other end of the table, just to be safe?"

"Ha ha, very funny. I'm going to short sheet your bed."

He closed the bathroom door. Only then would he allow a small smile. Minx. Her mischievous streak was going to make his orderly life hell. Again.

He'd been out of sorts since she'd disappeared, feeling adrift when he stopped working. He'd chalked it up to some kind of strange infatuation with a mysterious woman that he'd forget about soon enough. So he'd kept busy. And with recent news and the funeral this week, life had been more serious than usual.

Surya's sudden reappearance brought back a splash of color. This. He'd missed her vibrancy. It seemed to hold him by the neck and demand his attention. He wanted to explore why she affected him this way, why he was feeling so much lighter since walking into the suite, why knowing she was nearby made his heart clench.

He exhaled, shaking away the thoughts, then gave a low whistle at the sight of his surroundings. He was sure the bathroom was bigger than his small bedroom at home. The sink and counter stretched a mile long. The tub was a matching grey marble, tinted with gold. The shower area next to it could fit three or four people.

He looked at it longingly. Perhaps later tonight. Surya was sniffing at him like he'd been on a stuffy plane for over half a day. Which he had. He reached down and unzipped the side pocket of his carry-on, pulling out his bag of amenities. A cowboy wash and shave and a change of clothes would have to do for now. He needed to get his mind back on course to talk to Surya. He was sure she was an experienced translator between hostile negotiating parties, but he also needed to gauge her experience in locating and extracting prisoners. How good was she with weapons? He looked around again. Could she hike in a jungle? In those hot pink panties? No fucking way.

His body reacted to the image of Surya in those panties out in the Asian jungle. Mental groan. One ice-cold cowboy bath ahead.

* * * *

Dec clicked on the link. Jed McNeil's image popped up.

"Uncle JD. Really? A private video chat from a social media server?" he asked, incredulous.

Jed looked back at him solemnly. "Right now, other than face to face, it's more secure to talk to you via social media than on your phone."

That made Dec sit up. "Explain." He flicked some keys on the keyboard and critically surveyed the huge screen on the wall. "My end is secure. I would know if there's a bridge."

"Yes, but one of your agents communicating with you has a trojan in his. One that doesn't spread, but just collects data. The moles are piecing information by checking and comparing the location of each communication between your operatives. One call from where I am right now and they know you're on to them."

"I'll get my IT team on this," Dec said grimly. "Meanwhile, what do you have?"

"We've managed to get intel about a single missile sale exchanging hands on international waters by the Philippines. Abu Sayyef pirates run the piracy cartel there, so we're going to trace any sailing activity heading toward Bali from that area."

"Keep me posted. My guy just arrived in Bali. He checked in with me at the airport. Since he is not in my operations, his devices should be clean."

He watched Jed's light eyes glance off-screen, as if he was looking for confirmation from someone. He nodded and returned his attention to Dec. "Surya's chief says she will make sure of it."

"Is the interpreter just a front for other espionage duties, then?" Dec asked, a tad cynically. His file on GEM contract work showed mostly third-party interpreters and observers, such as contractors for the World Health Organization in third-world countries, concentrating mainly in areas where women and children were victims. Not that these areas were any less dangerous, since many of them were in some of the main hotspots of unrest. "I heard about a merger with your commando unit. That raised a few eyebrows, I'm sure, seeing that they're *just* interpreters."

Jed looked off-screen again, then back to him. "GEM operatives go where the commandos and SEAL teams can't go," he said simply. "Interpret that as you will."

"Who's that you're making eye contact with over there? Got a name for me?" Dec asked. He wanted to know more.

"T is the chief of operations for GEM. She wants you to know Surya and Kirk have worked together before, so they should be getting along in their hunt."

Dec frowned. "Kirk hasn't mentioned it."

"That's because he doesn't know her by that name. I'm sure he's recognized her by now." The corner of Jed's smile was faint. "GEM operatives are full of surprises that way."

Dec glanced at his watch. "I'll give Kirk a few hours to get his links and contacts set up before he calls. Should be interesting to hear the plans he and his partner have come up with. I'll let them know what you told me. It's unlikely he'll make any calls to any of my operatives."

"His cousin is your in-law," Jed pointed out quietly. "I'd check out all devices, Dec. No exceptions."

Dec nodded. There was a hacking technology which just needed a simple mobile call to be frequency-paired and the latest top-secret program released by DARPA was even more accurate and invasive. Because of his special contacts, his own securities agency was mostly protected with secured links. But DARPA—Defense Advanced Research Projects Agency—frequently worked with Jed's operatives who tended to move in and out of enemy as well as grey organizations. Jed's people thus had the ability to drop in on, and record, mobile conversations, such as missile sales between unsavory entities.

"Will do. Uncle JD it is then, if any of us has to contact you. You'll be hearing from my brother, Shane, regarding the SEALs waiting on hold. He might not be part of the operation, but these fellas are his friends and they'll help Shane. This is personal."

"I'm familiar with Hawk's team," Jed said. "I won't get in their way. Or Shane's. Unless necessary."

"Jed, you can take out the missile buyers. You can cancel any Russian assholes who have infiltrated the system, but you let the SEAL team handle the rogue SEALs. I want them back alive for myself. Shane and my brothers only allowed you to handle this because of the arrangement."

"Only if letting them live doesn't jeopardize the lives of others," Jed said, his voice remote. "You cannot make me guarantee giving them priority when they have hostages."

"Of course," Dec agreed, "but you know what I mean."

Jed nodded. "For your mother. I understand. I'll get those who have betrayed your trust. You'll keep your end of the agreement and share any information they have on their handlers. And all exchanges will be just between us, not with the departments. You let your Uncle JD do his job."

"Affirmative. Thank you for the call, Uncle JD."

Revenge. He had his and Jed had his own demons, except the latter played a long game in order to get the one he was after. Dec had no patience for that kind of game, had no desire for the big picture. He wanted to avenge his mother's death; with all his heart, he wished he could have foreseen the danger of enemies within. He wanted to crush those right *now*. The international scene—the big picture—could go to hell. The snakes in his yard first. For Mom. For his grieving dad. Everything else was secondary.

CHAPTER THREE

Kirk tried all the dishes, eating fast and efficiently. He couldn't take anything too spicy-hot, so he concentrated on the aromatic rice dishes. He was aware Surya was watching him with some amusement from across the table.

"Give me the names of these dishes," he said, pointing to the few he liked.

"That's nasi goreng. And lawar. The grilled skewered chicken is satay."

"Mmmm, I had that in a Malaysian restaurant in DC."

"The two countries have similar food," Surya told him. "They also both use Bahasa Melayu, although the local dialects are quite different."

"Why are you smiling like that?"

"Because of the way you eat. You cut the meat in half, pop it in your mouth, chew, swallow. Next. Did you even taste anything?"

Kirk paused in the middle of chewing. "Of course I did. I left all the spicy stuff for you."

She laughed, a soft, delightful sound. "Put in mouth. Chew. Spicy. Next. Put in mouth. Chew. Not spicy. Swallow. Put in mouth. Chew. Meat. Next. There is no pause in between to savor the dishes."

He took a drink of water, studying her. "This is food, not art. It's to fill my stomach. I enjoy what I eat and then move on. What's wrong with that?"

Surya cocked her head, her dark hair now back in a loose chignon, exposing that lovely neck that he'd been thinking of biting. Now, *that* he would savor. But he mustn't think of tasting her right now.

"You sound like a clockwork robot. How very boring. I'm going to have to loosen you up a little so you don't turn into a stuffy old shirt." She waved her fork at him. "It takes time and creativity to make a really good meal, you know. You didn't even stop to admire this beautiful table of food. I mean, you just attacked it like you're starving or something."

Kirk sat back in his chair. "I *am* starving," he said softly. "I've been starving—for answers from a certain woman, from frustration at not finding said woman. And then, when I do find her, I'm starved of time because there's this little emergency with hostages and a missile. So, my dilemma is, do I devour her quickly or do I keep her for later to enjoy? The thing is, she might disappear again, so what do I do?"

A hint of pink stained her dusky cheeks. She rested her chin on steepled fingers and they stared at each other like opponents.

"Are you suggesting that I am food?" she asked.

He shrugged. "Good food. You disappeared like really good food."

She blinked. "I'm not sure whether that's a compliment. The way you were treating really good food just now tells me you don't care what you eat." She waved a hand when he tried to interrupt. "Yes, I know we have a big job ahead of us and you're in a hurry."

"No, I'm saying I don't want you gone like a puff of smoke when we're done," he said. "I want you to be here at the end. Like dessert. I love dessert."

Her smile returned and those dark eyes gleamed back with laughter. "You know, maybe I was wrong. You do know how to eat right."

"Is it a deal?"

"What, about me being dessert? Oh, you mean disappearing on

you." She rolled her eyes. "I paid for this suite with my own hard-earned money. I'm not going to let a stupid missile interrupt my dream vacation."

Her odd sense of humor was what had attracted him when they met. She had a hilarious way of seeing everything revolving around her. Of course a missile wasn't going to stop her dream vacation.

"I'm glad you've got your priorities straight," Kirk noted dryly.

"Well, hey, look who's talking priorities. You want good dessert. I want a dream vacation."

They grinned at each other over the table, like kids playing silly games. He felt strangely light, as if a burden he'd been carrying had been lifted.

"So let's get this operation taken care of," he said. "I need an interpreter because my contacts have located a few locals who smuggle certain things into the forest. They're willing to talk but their dialect makes it difficult for quick questions about unusual activities."

"Not a problem. Jade brought me up to date with relevant details. I also made a few inquiries and found out why I'm needed when MacKenzie Securities has their own contractors. I'm sorry for your loss." Surya pushed back from her chair. "When you…umm…entered your room, I was getting it ready to make sure it was secured from external frequency interference. I just need your cell phone to pair with my device so it recognizes it as one with accepted numbers it won't jam."

"Okay."

"I've converted the TV and their cable for our video usage. You can speak to your boss without going through the channels. Ha ha, see what I did there?"

Shaking his head in amusement, Kirk stood up and followed her back to his room. She opened his closet and pulled out a small bag and he couldn't help admiring her cute ass as she headed for his bed. She turned, a little sly smile on her face.

"Bad idea. Let's go to your desk."

"You're such an imp."

"I know."

She opened the bag, taking out folders, small devices, and a laptop. His gaze rested on the small pieces of firearms.

"These have been tested. GPS units, walkie-talkies, receivers, compasses…and other stuff."

"Those small weapons won't be enough." They weren't going to fight the SEALs and their mercenaries, of course, but still, if they were caught in a battle, they weren't going to last very long with what she had in that bag. It did tell him she was comfortable with weapons, though.

"Bigger fire power on the way."

"How about a guide into the jungle, if needed?"

"I've hired a Malaysian man. He knows his way around."

"Do you personally know him?"

"Yes," she affirmed, "and I trust him."

"Can I meet with him?"

"Later, after you've talked to your locals." A small dimple appeared in her left cheek. "Gasi doesn't talk much but likes to eat, so if you're going to loosen his tongue, you'd better be buying a meal."

"Gasi," Kirk repeated.

"Short for Gergasi, which means giant." Surya casually assembled one of the small firearms into a more impressive one with what looked like plastic pieces. She tossed it at him and he caught it mid-air, testing its impressive lightness. She handed him one of the various parts on the table and at his soft whistle, she added, "Plastic guns. Hard to detect. 3-D printers are amazing and dangerous things."

"There's a lot more security because of the VIPs," he noted.

"Yeah. We have to be careful. These—" She pulled out more stuff. "—are our carrying cases."

Kirk examined them. "I hope the tampon box isn't for me," he deadpanned. "It'd seem odd when they pat me down and find it."

Surya showed him how the small gun fit into a fake bottom. "I suppose you can have the macho Batman drinking bottle," she said. "Now, a quick change of clothes and we're ready for our first tour."

"Should I arrange for a driver or have you taken care of that?"

"I'm driving."

He thought of the crazy traffic he'd experienced on the way from the airport. Those drivers were out and out nuts. "Nuh-uh. No way. I'm not putting my life in your hands out there."

She sniffed. "Don't be such a baby. Get changed and bring your baby bottle."

He snorted at her mockery. "Just don't drive like you have PMS," he retorted.

She laughed as she left his room. "Everybody here drives like they have PMS."

Kirk was afraid of that.

* * * *

Forty-five minutes later

Death by gun-toting hostiles sounded less frightening by the minute. These roads were a death trap, driven by people who seemed to think they were navigating bumper cars. He could feel the tension stretching across his shoulders and down his lower back as Surya swerved left to avoid a scooter, then right to keep from hitting an oncoming lorry. Nobody honked. Everyone was waving to each other.

"Driving Kirk Ryan, lalalalala. I think we should make a movie of that, with you gripping onto the dashboard with eyes as big as saucers while your female driver points out the beautiful sights in Bali. Look, to your left is—"

"Keep your eyes on the road!" Kirk gritted out.

"But I'm supposed to be showing you around," she protested. "You're missing the sights, with your face pressed against the windshield like that."

"I knew I shouldn't have let you drive," he muttered. He glanced over at her quickly. "I was listening to the instructions given by the concierge. All he said was "pooka" this and "poosing" that. There were no road names mentioned. How do you know you're going the right way?"

She shrugged. "I'm used to it here. It's spelled with a 'u'. 'Pusing' means 'turn'. He was saying 'puka', which is short for 'pusing kanan', to turn right. 'Pusing kiri' means to 'turn left'. He was quite clear."

"So he was just going 'go right' and 'go left'? That's ridiculous. We'll never get to the meeting place in the village this way." He could just see it now, reporting back to HQ and Declan he'd gotten lost and didn't have any information at all. "Surya—"

"Relax," she said in a soothing voice, which irritated him even more. "I got this."

"Surya!"

Kirk could only point at the car backing out of the driveway without stopping. He expelled a long string of expletives as he wiped the bead of sweat off his brow when Surya braked in time. It'd been a while since he'd used such language in front of anyone, especially a woman. After the offending car backed out and went its merry way, with the fucking driver waving at Surya, who waved back, he spat out a few more choice words, which earned him a laugh from the crazy woman beside him.

"You're turning me on, babe, with all those promises of fucking," she said. "Promise you'll give me some of that?"

She was such a tease. "How do you say turn around? 'Pusing'…what?"

Her forehead creased. "Why? Do you want me to turn the car around? Come on, we're almost there!"

"No, I want to say that in bed when we're fucking," he told her and smiled in satisfaction at her reaction. Two could play at teasing. "Well?"

"Just 'pusing' will do." She slanted him a look. "There's a small dialogue book in the door. Why don't you try learning a few phrases?"

He'd heard that GEM agents had a unique way of distracting their targets and getting them to do what they wanted. Just like that, Surya had provided him with a diversion from the madness on the road. For the next ten miles, he amused himself and her by reading phrases out loud, with her correcting his pronunciation. He knew she'd deliberately suggested the book to put him back on track. He liked to focus on something, to be in control of a situation by paying attention. She understood this about him, that being a troubleshooter, he didn't like not being able to fix a situation. Like watching people trying to kill each other on a road. Like feeling helpless a few days ago about the grief and anger enveloping the MacKenzies until this assignment offered him a way to put things right.

He liked that she understood this about him. It meant she'd been watching and had cared enough to notice. He made a note to monitor her closely, so he too would understand the stuff that made her tick. And oh, so she couldn't run off on him again as well.

* * * *

Surya snuck a peek at Kirk. He had that look on his face again. Total concentration, deep in thought. That look had both intrigued and frustrated her. She wanted that concentration on *her*, not some stupid problem he was trying to solve. On the other hand, she was afraid of that kind of attention because a man like that would take her apart and look too deeply. She could see it in the way he tackled a problem, in the care he took to get things done. He might be a CIA troubleshooter, but after reading up on the GEM files on him, she'd concluded Kirk Ryan was more just a CIA troubleshooter. He liked to fix problems to make people happy.

Like this assignment. She was sure he wasn't in it for money or for duty to the MacKenzies. Yes, he probably was after the bad guys with some revenge in mind, because this was a family tragedy, after all. However, there was a part of him—that deep focus—which was more interested in justice than the violence of revenge. Kirk liked to right a wrong. A fixer indeed.

Mary MacKenzie, from all accounts, sounded like someone well loved by all who entered her world. Kirk had given little snatches of details, enough for her to see how much he cared for his aunt-in-law. A beloved mother figure. That was such a strange notion in *her* world. Her family of sister-operatives was composed of independent creatures like her, brought together through the bond of being orphans, vagabonds and abandoned kids.

To have Kirk see and know her well meant exposing all her vulnerable parts. Surya shivered at the idea. She wasn't sure she wanted to share that much of herself. Yet, all that determined focus on her, giving her what she needed, just like that kiss earlier... Oh, boy, she really had it bad. She was thinking too much about the man.

"*Toonju kan sayer mana?*" Kirk interrupted her reverie. "Point where? Map is *peter?*"

"It's *tunjukan*. Show me where. *Tunjukan saya mana?*" she corrected. He was learning directions to get ready for his meeting with Gasi. She grinned. Yeah, total focus. "*Peta*, not peter. You're doing okay. How about a sentence?"

"Okay," he said, not looking up from his phrase book. "How much longer to the village?"

"Fifteen minutes."

"Lima belas," he said in Malay.

"Not like lima beans. It's pronounced *lee*-ma. *Lima belas minit.*"

"*Toonju-kan saya peter dimana lima belas minit.* You're laughing. What's so funny? I asked you to show me on the map where we are in fifteen minutes."

Surya laughed so hard, she had to slow down to wipe the tears from her eyes. Fortunately, the road had very few cars at the moment.

"No, you asked me to show you where your peter is going in fifteen minutes," she told him, then broke out in merriment again.

After a moment, he joined her, his deep male laughter filling the car. It felt good to laugh together. It never ceased to surprise her how comfortable she was with him. Sure, there was that delicious sexual tension, of being aware of, and attracted to, a fine male specimen. And he *was* fine—six foot two, lean and hard-bodied, with that nice, easy smile and those deep-set, knowing blue eyes which were always assessing. He wore that easy demeanor she'd seen in psychologists and scammers—the one that engaged people in conversations to reveal clues about themselves. She was sure he saw himself more the former than the latter, but his job as a troubleshooter must include a few scams here and there.

But even knowing he was analyzing her didn't make her feel

uncomfortable. Maybe it was the challenge to keep him guessing. Maybe it was the attraction—that determined glint she caught in his eyes now and then was thrilling and a little scary. She wasn't sure what she really wanted with this man. Her lifestyle since joining GEM had been simple—living the high life was way better than living on the streets. It was her mantra. She didn't mind the dangerous situations—hell, she'd grown up fending for herself in the most dangerous places—but now she had money and security. Now, when she wanted to, she could join her GEM sisters for family-type excursions. Now, she could save money and, if she wanted to, she could spend it on holiday pampering, fulfilling her need to live in luxury.

It'd been years since her days scampering in the dirt, digging through the mountainous piles of trash for her next meal, and finding shelter away from the street gangs. But a part of her was still that child, one who dreamed about living the life she now had. And Surya liked pampering that little wild girl. She glanced at the man beside her again. A relationship with him promised to be complicated and she wasn't sure whether she was ready to drop her mantra.

"We're here," she told him, navigating the car into a dusty side street. "What did your contacts tell you to do?"

"The two villagers will see us inside one of the shops. Here's the name of the place. I'm assuming there is some sort of downtown-type area where the shops are located?"

Surya looked at the paper. "This village is in the interior of Bali by the rainforest. Says here to go into the shops and ask for directions to another village. Okay, I know where it's referring to. There's the most magnificent rainforest resort in the other place, so everyone would be used to visitors dropping by asking questions or directions."

"Okay. What's the name of the resort?"

"Awang Awang. It's amazing." Surya sighed. Now, that was where she should spend her next vacation. "It's totally set up in the mountains looking down at the rainforests. It's a dream place if you want to escape from the usual hustle and bustle."

Kirk frowned. "No wonder my contacts brought that to my

attention. If it's a touristy mecca, why would these villagers notice any unusual activities with strangers? There would be plenty of people making trips into the rainforests, right?" He stroked his chin. "Hmm. You'd think Bali jungles would be the last place for a terrorist hideout. They're usually deep in the Sulawesi islands."

Surya parked the car on a street corner. "Well, these aren't just terrorists," she pointed out. "They are Caucasians walking in and out of the rainforest. Your bad SEALs and turncoat operatives wouldn't look too suspicious hiking around the fabulous resort."

"Good point." He opened the car door. "Ready?"

"Yeah."

* * * *

Not far away

"Vadim, we heard Petrovich is dead." Mark Walters didn't add he was glad the bastard was dead. He loosened his grip on his cell phone, trying not to betray his tension. "They got Holland."

"Do you think I wouldn't know about this?"

"Holland is going to name names. MacKenzie's going to send his men after us."

He knew he was up shit creek. It didn't matter. It was over for him, but he needed to make sure his family was taken care of. Petrovich had had him in a stranglehold, but with him dead, there was hope Vadim would be a bit more humane. He closed his eyes. His beautiful wife and his baby.

"We're keeping an eye on such matters," Vadim replied. "We've got people inside, you know. Holland isn't sure of our other insiders, so you're safe for now. They're busy grieving. If they make a move, we'll just kill another one of them. We'll keep them busy with funerals."

The cold laughter that followed the threat made him swallow. Him, a SEAL. He was supposed to be the warrior here, and yet these fucking men had reduced him to a frightened man, unable to think, by killing the people close to him.

"Look, that's all fine, but the five of us aren't going to be able to keep these fucking militants from shooting that missile at the Interpol General Assembly. This whole thing went to shit with Petrovich's death. Who's going to pay the ransom these militants are demanding? Your people? You've kept us in the dark long enough. We need information to proceed."

"You'll do as you're told, or have you forgotten your family is also under our surveillance?"

His eyes shot open. He could feel his heart rate increase. He made his voice softer. "Don't hurt them, please. Look, I've done everything you've told me. I can only count on my SEAL buddy. The other three, they're fucking mercenaries, so their loyalties aren't exactly their best trait. They'll just go along with the terrorists, collect the money, and cut and run."

"This is laughable. Your loyalty? You have no loyalty right now."

He could cry at his loss. This was his life and he'd really, really messed up. All he could do now was make sure his wife and baby would live. One of them was going to kill him in the end—these fuckers, the terrorists, the MacKenzies. It didn't matter which side. He was surrounded.

"Look, Vadim, I know I'm nothing to you," he placated, "but if you want me to find where they're hiding our scientists, at least let me in on the details. I've done as we were ordered but look what happened when you didn't give us enough information to make sure everything went your way. We lured both of them while they were meeting here for Petrovich, after seeking permission with these militants to use their territory. But because you didn't tell me about Petrovich's death, they've now changed the game plan and fucking moved the prisoners from under our noses. They know their way around the forests here more than we do. The five of us are searching like blind men looking for a needle. Asking the locals questions has been a delicate operation. And even if we do locate them, I repeat, how are we going to stop this missile?"

"We do not care about the missile."

His mind went silent as he grasped the reality of what was happening—would happen in a matter of days. "Fuck, man, we can't just let them fire it towards the assembly. Hundreds of people might be killed!"

"That isn't your business. Your job now is to find their fucking hiding hole and get our scientists back. Your job wasn't supposed to lose them in the first place."

"*My* job was done! We were to hold on to the hostages until Petrovich flew over with the money. It's all a SNAFU right now, what with angry militants, a missile crisis, and no money for the mercs, whom *you* hired, might I add. I have my hands full trying to convince everyone to follow orders as it is. I know the MacKenzies. They aren't just going to sit home and cry. They have plans and if they aren't implemented by now, they are being implemented. It's just a matter of time before they find out who else besides Holland you have in your pocket, Vadim."

"You're bold. Petrovich would never let you talk back to him like this. Are you questioning my judgment?"

"No, Sir. I'm trying to explain to you the direness of the situation. I'm just waiting for your next instructions." He tried very hard to keep the sarcasm out of his voice. At this point, his patience was hanging on by a thread. "Like I said before, asking the villagers too many questions will raise suspicions, even in a tourist area this side of the boonies."

"All right. I'll give you some information since you're working against the clock," Vadim conceded. "The militants have contacted the US government demanding ransom for the hostages. I'm sure there are other stipulations, but they're of no interest to me. They've threatened to shoot a rocket right into the heart of the Interpol Assembly if their terms aren't met. So, as the usual protocol goes, they'll be sending an intermediary to negotiate stupid, but necessary, details such as where, when, and how the exchange will be made. I suggest you look for that person asking the same questions you have at your end and follow him. That would lead you to our scientists. Eliminate the intermediary once the exchange has been made and get the prisoners back in your hands. Contact me then."

"Wait. Now you want me to look for some intermediary the government has sent? I don't even have a face or name now! Where do I fucking start?"

"That is your problem. You know the consequences, Mark. Do this and you can take your little family and disappear."

He knew fucking well Vadim and his gang of moles weren't going to just let him disappear. He was prepared to die, but first he had to take care of a few things to ensure his family was safe. He couldn't save himself, not now, not after he'd realized his actions had gotten Mary MacKenzie murdered, but he'd do everything in his power to protect his wife and baby.

"And the missile?" he asked, already knowing the answer.

"That isn't your problem. We're only interested in the two scientists. Get them and let the terrorists fight over the cash the CIA's prepared to pay. It's even better since we don't have to spend a single dime and everyone will blame the Abu Sayyeh gang for the fallout. We've already paid for everything you've requested—cash, the boat, the ammo. What kind of SEALs lose their prisoners? That rocket on their little island is the CIA's problem. We're just lucky we decided not to keep the scientists there, like they suggested. Now, get them before they're moved to that island. Are we clear so far?"

"Crystal," Mark replied, bitterly. The lives of hundreds on his conscience, that was what was clear. His local contacts helping him to get directions to the forbidden territories better be good. "I'll contact you when I have the scientists."

He ended the call and walked to his vehicle, which he'd just filled with supplies for the team. Team Fucked-Up, that was what they were. He felt alone and lost. And angry at Holland. He didn't know what had happened back in the States but that phone call from Justin had put him in full panic mode. Holland had somehow gotten Petrovich into the compound and helped kidnap Mrs. MacKenzie. Perhaps the stupid asshole didn't know she would be killed, but still. They were in this sorry state because of their families' lives being threatened, but he hoped he'd have drawn the line at killing MacKenzie women or children.

Mark smashed his fist hard against the car, denting the hood. He couldn't stand here like a fool full of regrets now. He'd do what he must do. First, he had to make a quick call to his cousin and hope he'd keep his promise from long ago to protect Shelly if he didn't make it. He didn't want to say goodbye to his wife. Her phone might be monitored by those bastards. After that, he'd deliver the bad news to the others and see if he could convince the mercs to hang on for one more op.

CHAPTER FOUR

"Kirk, I think we should wait until we see Gasi tonight before tracking in there," Surya said. "Besides, I'm hungry."

Kirk looked down the dusty path leading into the rain forest. It was well-used by the locals and the two they'd just interviewed assured him many tourists trekked down it too. There was a small flourishing open-air market and, although it was late in the day, a few stands were open, attracting some tourists who had opted to take a walk in the cooler hours.

Watching Surya questioning them had been a revelation too. She'd wiped off her lipstick and taken off her earrings. She'd buttoned up her shirt. Hell, she'd even changed her walk, putting a little distance between them. It was fascinating how she'd morphed into someone else before his eyes. Her voice was soft and lyrical as she spoke in *Melayu* to the two villagers, making them laugh with a line here and there. She had an easy smile on her face as she interpreted his questions in between her chatter. He could tell she was taking time loosening them up, telling them some kind of story until their faces became more animated and their demeanor turned more familiar. GEM contractors had a great reputation for working within foreign countries and were often an integral part of the social teams in organizations such as the World Health Organization and Doctors Without Borders. He wondered about her background, because she looked so natural in this setting.

"Why buy supplies here?" Kirk asked, frowning. "I understand it won't catch anyone's attention when two or three Caucasians shop around and walk in and out of the woods and all, but it's still odd. Why don't the terrorists send their own people to get supplies? Surely they would look even less conspicuous, hauling that much food?"

"Good question. It's a good tactic, though. While they are negotiating to release the prisoners, the mercenaries guard the hostages somewhere no one expected," Surya said. "Sort of distracting the enemy—rocket in one place, hostages another, negotiation, another."

He mulled that over for a few seconds. It did make good strategic sense. If Surya's theory was correct, he would have to tell Dec to coordinate at least two groups of SEALs for the operations ahead. How else could they track the whereabouts of the missile and rescue the scientists when they were at different locations? He would be busy in the middle of negotiating with the kidnappers and if they proved to be as cutthroat as their reputation, they'd be signaling to dump the dead scientists somewhere while pretending to agree with him about the terms and monetary exchange. Somehow, he must improve the odds of getting to the scientists while they were alive. The only way to do this was to do some tracking. He hoped this friend of Surya—Gasi—was as good as she said.

"Agreed," he said. "I need to talk to my operations chief as well as Dec first anyway. They need to track our location."

Surya tapped his water bottle. "Done. Duh. Did you forget we brought some toys?"

Kirk smiled. "I didn't, but I prefer talk before action in this case because so many people are involved."

Surya cocked her head. "Hopefully you have more action in mind later." She gave him a sweet smile and added, "Although talking can be fun. Like foreplay."

"I heard jungle sex is fun," he bantered.

Surya shuddered. "That is so not what I have in mind."

He couldn't help teasing her, even while he was taking out his phone to dial Dec's number. "You'll never know until you try it. Wild monkey sex is—uh, it's me. Is our link secured?"

No names in public. He opened the car door and slipped inside. Surya tapped the window and pointed toward the market. He assumed she wanted to walk around and check it out and nodded in agreement. Wiping away the perspiration on his forehead, he turned on the air conditioning.

"Yes," Dec replied on the other end. "Give me what you got."

"I have a lead," Kirk began, and then gave a quick but detailed summary. He also provided their current location before cautioning he wasn't a hundred percent. "The villagers' observations are just that, observations. But they're locals and very used to foreign visitors and their habits. Tourists buying too much food and supplies would catch their attention. Carrying the supplies into the forest during late evening hours is also suspicious. In the last few days, two have asked questions about guides into territory the locals said were dangerous. That's also interesting."

"It's a good lead. What is the overall SITREP?"

"It's not going to be easy," Kirk replied. The situation was alarmingly serious. "I received communication from my supervisor on where the kidnappers want to negotiate. It's about ten miles from here, which is another clue to our scientists being in the jungle near this village. That makes two different locations."

"And then there's the missile in a third place," Dec added.

"That's right," he agreed. "Three different problems."

Dec was silent for a few seconds. Then he said, "Hawk's SEAL team will go to the jungle. We need more info about those dangerous territories you were talking about. You take over the negotiations and keep in contact. Wear the earpiece so you know what is taking place at the other locations."

"Surya has a guide I can talk to about those areas. We're meeting soon."

"How's working with the GEM translator working out?"

Kirk looked toward the marketplace. There weren't too many people about at this hour, so it was easy to find Surya. She was talking to several youths standing at the edge of the stalls. One of them pointed to the path leading into the woods. With her coloring she looked very natural out there.

"It's working out fine," he replied, frowning slightly when one of the male youths walked closer to her. What was she asking those kids?

"Jed informed me you know her."

Kirk sighed. Of course someone would inform Dec. Dec always knew things. "Yeah," he admitted and didn't volunteer any details.

"That bad, huh?"

"I...we...Dec, she and I will be okay, if you're worried we aren't getting along," Kirk said, and hurriedly added, "She's excellent at her job."

"That good, huh?"

He could hear the smile in Dec's voice. "How much did McNeil tell you?" he demanded.

"Just that you've been looking for her for a while."

He wondered again about Declan and McNeil. How well did they know each other that they would talk about him and his knowing Surya? It wasn't the kind of conversation in which he could picture the Ice Man.

"Just checking to make sure things are running smoothly, that's all," Dec continued.

"So far, she's been very helpful," Kirk said, keeping to the operations side of things. "Translation, a guide, local sight-seeing. If you're sending Hawk's team in, how are they going to show up in the middle of the jungle without permission?"

"Your cousin is also a SEAL, Kirk. Surely you know by now they'll show up any way they want to," Dec replied, dryly.

By sea, air, and land. In his family, he'd grown up listening to stories about the Navy SEALs and their prowess. He'd seen some of the things his cousin and his team had done.

"They'll still need a more specific location to show up in," Kirk pointed out. "The jungles around here are miles deep."

Surya was walking a bit farther away with that kid than he would like. He'd better get out there to see what she was up to.

"Hopefully, you can obtain that soon. Make the negotiations, see if there are any non-Asians among them. If you could identify the person in charge of the hostages, we'll have someone follow him. Do your usual thing—get confirmation they're alive—a call, live feed—anything from which we could trace a signal. The SEALs are already waiting for our signal."

Kirk sat up in his seat. "They're here?"

"Close by."

Ah. They were underwater. Waiting. Good to know.

"What about the missile?"

"Jed's people know about the delivery. I'm assuming they're tracking it on satellite and are on top of things at that end. I'll be sending in one of my teams, maybe even join in the hunt. Shane's coordinating that operation. Not being able to do anything with chasing down the traitors is driving him nuts, so this is helping him deal. Since the rocket crisis has nothing to do with the Russian assholes, those fuckers don't know any of my men, so I can get to them without jeopardizing your mission."

"Sounds good. It looks like I'm the one who has to start all the action," Kirk said with a slight smile as he turned off the air and got out of the car. "I like being the nerdy negotiator guy playing such an important role among you action maniacs."

There were sounds of shouting from where Surya had headed. He broke into a slow run.

"Sounds like you're getting some action at your end."

"Nothing I can't handle."

"Call me back ASAP. We active maniacs are antsy."

"Soon," Kirk said, trying not to sound too urgent. "But I need to catch up with Surya. Now."

He swore he heard Dec give a chuckle but couldn't tell since he was running. Surya and some big guy were talking loudly at each other.

"From what Jed told me about your run-in with her, good luck."

Kirk slipped the cell into his pocket as he slowed down a bit. Surya. Kids, a few of them looked more like older teens. Two big-ass dudes. He took a deep breath, not wanting to look too much in a hurry. Shouting now by one of the guys. The kids milling around and talking all at once. Surya looking upset and afraid. Surya. Looking afraid. His suspicion meter went up several notches.

"Just give me back my wallet!" the big guy ordered loudly. He turned left and right, addressing the kids. "One of you has it. You better give it back or else!"

"Lady, quit hiding that kid behind you. She's the one who picked my pocket," the other man ordered.

"How dare you accuse my friend of doing such a thing?" Surya put her hands on her hips. She was speaking with a local accent. "Just stop shouting. You're frightening the children."

"These kids are pro pickpocket gangs. Their surrounding and bumping us weren't an accident. That one put her hand in my pocket and took something important. And another one has my friend's wallet. I said give them back or you'll regret it, friend or not."

Kirk was fifteen feet away and about to insert himself into the situation when another voice interrupted from behind him.

"What's going on?"

He turned. Another man was heading toward the group, his face grim, a heavy backpack slung over one shoulder. He passed Kirk without acknowledging him.

"You guys didn't come out to meet me," the man said, his voice quiet. "What's the delay?"

"These kids. They surrounded us and picked our pockets. Now this chick is interfering when we want to get Rob's wallet back. And that one. That one took my flashlight and stuff from my back pocket."

The new guy looked around. "I told you to be careful with the kids. They're mostly orphans looking for a quick victim. Don't tell me you wusses let them come that close. Hey, miss, sorry, but can you ask these kids for our stuff back? Look, I'll reward them with food and some money. We're just hikers here and really need our IDs back. Please?"

His tone was casual but his stance was alert. He'd deliberately placed himself between the first two men and Surya.

"Well…" Surya said, giving them a considering look.

"Well, what?" One of the others took a step forward. "I'm through being nice. Why don't you hand over that kid before I show you how—"

"Rob, why don't you get the other stuff from the car?" the man with the backpack interrupted. "We need to get started hiking back because we don't want it to get too late. Know what I mean? Let me handle this."

His voice was firm, like someone who was in charge.

His friend hesitated for a second. "Sure. You just get our belongings back from these thieves. Fu—"

"No cussing in public," the man interrupted again. "Come on, dudes, you know the rules." When the two guys reluctantly went off, he turned back to Surya and smiled apologetically, "We're really in a hurry, miss. Don't be scared. My friends are just upset about their wallets. Here, see? I have some chocolate for the children."

Kirk watched him pull out some candy bars from his cargo pants and they were instantly grabbed by a few of the kids nearby. He noticed the quick way he swatted off a few of the hands from his body, making sure his own pockets weren't being picked. Instead of walking any closer to the group, Kirk decided to hang back at one of the stalls and play spectator. He didn't want to get in the way of whatever Surya was doing.

"Okay, I'll help because you're a nice man," Surya said. She turned and spoke to the kids in their language before two pulled out things from their pockets and showed them to her. She took them and examined them. "Wallet, ID, map, and flashlight. Right, mister? They say this is all the stuff but you must give them food, like you promised."

"Of course. Here, let me set down my backpack on the table over there so I can get the food out. Now, I don't want any of the kids to come near me while I'm doing it, okay?"

Again, Kirk noted the easy yet careful demeanor of the man as he stationed himself at the table, facing the kids. From his vantage point, he could see the newcomer. Probably mid-to-late twenties, dressed in a tee and cargo pants with hiking shoes, backward cap on, he looked like a regular tourist hiker, one of many in the area enjoying the trails set up for visitors. But the watchfulness in his eyes and the way he was handling the situation were telling. Even as he unzipped his backpack and pulled out food items—cans, plastic bags—his gaze never left the kids. His smile never reached his eyes.

"Here you go, miss," he said, pushing the items forward. "Why don't you come get them and just set my friends' stuff down on the table? Fair exchange, right?"

Surya walked over after giving the kids an order. At her soft words, the latter hung back. Like him, they stood watching Surya.

"How about a few more cans?" she asked after a moment. "You look a lot less hungry than these kids. Look at those big arms and compare them to their skinny little ones."

Kirk grinned. She would make a fine negotiator.

"You drive a hard bargain, lady. You're a good friend to have," the younger man said as he dug in and pulled out a few more cans.

Surya shrugged. "That's what friends are for. We stick together, especially in times of trouble."

Kirk looked on thoughtfully as the man froze and there was a long moment of silence. Surya didn't appear to notice, fiddling with the cans and throwing them one by one to the waiting kids nearby.

"Stick together in times of trouble," he repeated slowly.

"True, no?" Surya asked. "Well, then, here's your friends' stuff. I take care of my friends and you take care of yours."

The man gave a short bark of laughter. It sounded humorless to Kirk. He zipped everything up and hefted the strap to the bundle onto his shoulder again.

"Where were you when I needed to hear that?" he asked as he walked around the table. "Here come my friends."

"I go now," Surya said. "I don't like them as much as I like you. I think you're a better friend than them. *Selamat malam.*"

She walked off back in the direction of the kids. Throughout the whole incident, she did not once acknowledge Kirk, although he was sure she was aware he was within calling distance.

The youths and kids milled around her excitedly, all of them happy with their "loot." Kirk knew the number one problem among poor Indonesian children was malnutrition, especially in the rural areas. The food items were going to take care of some hungry kids tonight and all because of Surya being there. A wave of tenderness filled him as realization dawned. She was a GEM operative, often working among camps and international social services in Third World countries. She knew exactly how to handle this type of situation because she understood what was wanted and needed. She'd seen enough poverty to know what to negotiate for, instead of the usual shouting back at angry tourists. With just a few well-chosen words, she'd conveyed to the stranger the children's plight and he'd willingly parted with more of his food.

He frowned as he continued looking at the fast disappearing trio of men. They were all carrying backpacks. The two who had been more aggressive were gesturing and talking, still upset. The one who'd talked to Surya said something that appeared to shut the conversation down. As they were about to disappear into the shadows, one of them bent over, picked up what looked like a rock, and threw it back toward the kids. He shouted something Kirk couldn't make out but he could imagine what the expletive was. Okay, maybe Surya wouldn't have been quite as successful placating those two.

After a few minutes, Surya waved goodbye to her new friends and started back toward the car, with Kirk following.

When he joined her in the car, she gave him that sly smile he was now familiar with. Like the cat who stole the cream. Oh, yes, his girl had a secret. He was both intrigued and mildly amused. Here he was, on assignment, and the woman was getting in on it like a boss.

He waved his smart phone at her. *"Perempuan jahat!"* he announced.

Her grin widened. "Doing translation, eh?"

"Since you're doing such a good job being a negotiator, I thought I'd better brush up on my translation services," he told her solemnly. "It says here, that's Bahasa for 'hellcat'."

She chuckled as she started up the car. "I suppose that's one translation. Usually it means mischievous or wicked." She stepped on the gas pedal, rumbling the engine, and gave him a teasing look. "Ready to get back on the road, scaredy cat?"

Kirk gave her a side glance. "Wicked. Yeah, that describes you. You gonna tell me what you were up to back there with our suspects?"

"Ahhh. You figured it out already."

He sniffed. "What's hard about that? He walked like a damn military man."

"Mmm-hmm. Big muscular arms. And so strong. He was carrying that backpack like it weighed nothing. Too bad he's the bad SEAL."

"How do you know he's the SEAL and not one of the mercenaries?" Kirk asked, curious.

"There was a small SEAL trident tattoo on his wrist. I saw it when he handed me the cans. The other two men were rougher and their bodies were bulkier. They do have military training, though. I can tell from the way they moved and their body language. It's just that the SEAL was a lot more attentive to details."

"All that in the few minutes shouting at the first two men and another few haggling with the one who came up later, huh?"

"Yup. But I cheated. I asked the older kids about men going in and out of the woods who were hiking with too many supplies. They told me about the tough guys bringing loads into the forest at night. They'd planned to pick their pockets for cash because they were hungry. So…" Surya shrugged. "I thought I'd help them out."

Kirk shook his head. She was something else. "Most people help by giving the kids cash, you know," he said, "and not by encouraging a life of crime."

Surya dimpled back at him. "I wanted to see them in action. Brings back old memories."

He cocked an eyebrow. "Memories? As in…you were a child pickpocket?"

Surya laughed softly. "Hard to believe, huh? I was the best before I was adopted." She looked whimsical for a second. "Dirty, hungry, and needy all the time. Tourists eating left and right, tempting us with all that cash in their pockets. It's getting harder, you know, what with the wide usage of credit cards. Child pickpockets are now part of real gangs with head gangsters who take their stolen cards in exchange for money. The kids are often treated badly. Back in my day, you could be a lone agent, doing your own little thing. Not any more."

Kirk couldn't imagine Surya as a dirty little kid, but he could see her picking pockets. She was very good at stealing his things, if memory served him right.

"So, you got close to the people we're looking for," he said. "Not sure if that's a good idea."

"I didn't plan it that way. I'd actually wanted to just watch the kids steal the wallets and then take a look at what's in them, but those men had their antennae up the moment the kids swarmed around them. I had to jump in or they would have caught the girl and who knows whether they're the kid-beating kind of guys?" She looked angry. "I wasn't going to see children get hurt, so I stepped in. Then that younger man appeared. He seemed in charge, so I guess that's a good thing or they might not have listened to him."

She took a turn and they were on a dusty road, off the streets.

"Where are we going?"

She glanced at him. "Gasi's place isn't far. I tagged the wallet and flashlight, so we can actually trail them to wherever they're heading. There was a map of some kind, so I'm thinking they have all those supplies because they're heading for that forbidden territory we heard about. Do you think they have the scientists there?"

"Wait, hold up." Kirk pinched his nose. "That was a lot of stuff in that answer. You tagged those guys."

Surya grinned at him. "Yeah," she replied. "It's a GPS-like tag, but only sends intermittent signals to save battery and avoid detection. We can't trail after them immediately. He's a SEAL and besides, they're professionals. They'll know if we're too close to them. Sound carries in the woods, you know. When they come to a stop, I'll get the last signal and we can head there. That way, there'll always be enough distance between us. So, we need Gasi ASAP."

Kirk shook his head. "We can't take out that team all by ourselves, sweetheart. We have to get the SEAL team Dec MacKenzie has set up to do this part."

"We aren't going to 'take them on'. We're just following them to get the right location for the SEAL team. How else would they know where to go? If we wait for your friends to arrive, they could be too far in that forest for us to track. This way, we follow far enough to mark the right spot. That's why Gasi is important. He'll know exactly how to track quickly and also give us landmarks to send to your SEALs."

Kirk stared out of the windshield, half-taking in the very scenic route of green, green trees in between paddy fields. Timing and planning were two very important elements of negotiations. This one was particularly tricky because the bad guys had a history of not keeping their word. They had a rocket, which they might or might not shoot, even if they received the ransom. They had hostages, whom they might or might not release, for the same reason. Usually, the terrorists only executed one threat at a time; this double threat was a bit odd, to say the least. Either one would be enough to garner attention, but they'd chosen to make this a private demand, without any news leakage. Which was fine with his side, what with an international meeting taking place.

"What are you thinking? You've had that look on your face before," Surya noted.

"What look?" He turned his attention back to her.

Her smile was slow, her eyes twinkling with mischief. "When I tied you up and spanked you. You have the same look now. Very determined, like a man on a mission."

He narrowed his eyes at her. "Yeah." He remembered his exact thoughts then. "I was thinking of exacting similar revenge when I found you, with some extra punishment."

"It was only a couple of very light smacks!" she protested. "Your bare butt was tempting, that's all. You should forgive and forget."

He put his hand on her knee and squeezed lightly. He felt her slight shiver.

"So much to think about for after this adventure," he said. The sexy come-hither look in her eyes made him hot again, even though the air in the car was cool. He wanted to lean over and kiss those lips. He ran his hand over her thigh before changing the subject back to their current problem. "I was wondering about the SEALs who had turned on the MacKenzies."

"Well, we know the one they caught—Holland, wasn't it?—told them they were going to hurt his family. I'm assuming these turncoats are also following orders because of Petrovich's threats. That's why I said what I said back there, just to test his reaction."

He liked having a partner who could jump back and forth with his thoughts so seamlessly. He remembered how he'd missed her when she left him. That quick wit. The way she connected his ideas and also brought in her own. He wondered if she felt the same connection with him. Obviously not, because she'd disappeared. He tamped down the disappointment. He *would* convince her later, but now they had to strategize.

"The thing is, these guys lured our scientists for the Russian moles, right?" he continued. "According to Declan, the current situation is their Plan B because Petrovich died without paying the terrorists off. So, why are these SEALs here, guarding prisoners, if they were no longer under threat? They have to know Petrovich is dead or the demand for ransom wouldn't make sense."

"So there is a new Russian handler who took Petrovich's place. That's nothing new. They have been hidden in our system for at least ten years, Kirk."

Kirk nodded. "I know, but something still doesn't feel right."

Surya chewed on her lip. After a few seconds, she said, "Agreed. Why isn't the new Russian handler paying them off? We know the Russians really wanted the scientists."

"That's exactly what's bothering me."

"We're almost at Gasi's," Surya said. "I'll keep mulling this over while we get ready for our short trek."

"I'll make another quick call to Dec to make sure he gets our signals to the SEALs who are waiting."

"Where are they waiting?" Surya asked.

He pointed east. "It's all islands here, babe. They're SEALs, so they're either on a ship or to be even closer, they're in some kind of pod nearby."

She made a turn and he could see a small hut at the end of the dirt driveway. She flashed her beams several times.

"SEALs hunting SEALs," Surya murmured. "It's so sad. And there's Gasi waiting for me."

Kirk leaned forward to check out this guide about whom Surya kept talking. It took him a few long seconds to make out the lone figure standing on a rock. He was leaning on a very big stick, camouflaged in brown and green attire.

Kirk turned. "He's...ah...very short for a man nicknamed Giant."

Surya laughed.

CHAPTER FIVE

Two hours later

Perspiration popped out of Kirk, drenching his clothes. He took a swig from his container. Looking ahead, he saw his guide and his translator, moving through the forest as if they didn't notice the humidity. Come on. Surely they felt as if their pores were the size of nostrils too.

"Four-foot-four to your six-foot-two, sweetheart," Surya had informed him. "Don't bring it up or he'll beat you with that stick. He's very, very good with it. He knows Silat."

Silat was the martial art around this part of the world. Kirk recalled having seen it performed on a video before. So, that told him Gasi was in very good shape.

So was Surya, from the way she was keeping up with the short guy. But the operative word was *sweetheart*. Surya had called him sweetheart.

Right now, hiking in the dark of the jungle, with Gasi in front, poking with his big stick to make sure there weren't any sleeping snakes, he shouldn't be thinking about that. He should be looking for them too. He wasn't particularly fond of snakes, especially when they were big and hungry. But she looked so tempting in that brown and green outfit. It wasn't camo gear, since they didn't want to draw any attention. More like hiking attire. She had everything packed in the trunk, in the tire compartment, and it had only taken them half an hour to get ready at Gasi's.

To be honest, he hadn't been sure whether Surya was the jungle-hiking type. He'd seen her running around in mind-boggling high heels, but roughing it? Now, here she was, moving silently in the greenery, a *parang*—machete—in one hand, a headlamp—which somehow managed to make her look fashionable and adorably sexy—banded around her forehead, as if she'd done this before.

Gasi had told them, from the few pinpoints of red that pinged back from the remote tag, he knew where they were headed. It seemed that the villagers were not the only ones who set "illegal" fires in the jungle to clear land for their farming. The "forbidden territories" was just local lingo for where terrorists had taken over. The latter had cleared certain areas for their own encampments, using the area for weapons distribution and perhaps hostage prisons. Villagers avoided those areas and kept mum about them to the authorities because of the trouble these terrorists caused to their families and farmland. Besides, the government was after them for the illegal fires, so reporting on the gangsters would mean a stop to their own way of life.

His satellite phone was high end, but it needed to be pointed to the sky to connect a call. Not possible under this green umbrella. He could make a call when they reached a clearing or a river, as Gasi said there were several nearby. He did, however, have a connected pager and it had successfully sent two quick messages for him. Dec should be tracking him through them by now and directing the SEALs coming their way. There were several big rivers in this area. He was sure the SEAL team had studied and would know the best one to take. He'd read about one of the supersecret stealth boats some SEAL teams had been using that wouldn't register on any commercial radar. They were designed to navigate shorelines and rivers. Perhaps Hawk's team would arrive in one of those.

In his short message, he'd mentioned forbidden zones in deforested areas of the island. Dec, maybe with the help of McNeil, should be able to get high-resolution satellite images to identify possible locations. That would increase the chances of discovery exponentially.

His last message reiterated Surya's and his plan. "Once location of prisoners is confirmed, we'll plant target signal boost. Then we leave." The SEALs would handle it from there while his own small team of three headed back to the car. After that, with a short rest, he would prepare to meet for negotiations. If the SEALs arrived at the target and their operation was successful, he would hold an ace in his pocket. Then there would only be the rocket to worry about.

Gasi stopped and looked back. The light from his headlamp splashed in Kirk's direction, making him squint until the guide adjusted the brightness.

"This spot. Last red signal blink-blink," he told them quietly.

"Okay," Surya said. She turned to Kirk. "They shouldn't be too far from here."

Kirk peered into the darkness. "I need to get close to the river so we can plant the signal. Then we'll leave."

"Gasi?"

The guide pointed in one direction. Kirk saw only shadows and branches.

"There," Gasi said. "But that's very, very close. I can smell smoke. That means it's near where they cleared land."

Yes, Kirk could smell the acridness hanging in the air too. Fire from deforestation had been a major contributor of decreased air quality in Indonesia. The smell of smoke sometimes could overwhelm a whole island, especially when there was no rain.

"Let's go close enough where I can see it," he said. "I need a clearing or the river to send with the satellite phone. One of us can plant the device while the other makes sure the feed is working properly. Shouldn't take more than a minute."

"Right," Surya replied. "I'll do it while you test the satellite phone. Gasi, you stand guard."

Someone had cleared a path through the thicket and the progress was easier. It didn't look like a freshly made path, though. If they were really entering a forbidden territory, then this must be used by the Abu Sayyeh terrorists. It only emphasized how close they were to danger. He tapped Surya's shoulder.

"Be careful," he mouthed.

She gave him a thumbs-up. "In and out," she said, and winked at him.

The clearing appeared behind a big clump, like an unexpected shadowy ribbon. The glow of moonlight and starlight made everything visually clear. After a moment or two, he could make out shapes that weren't part of nature. A dock? Some kind of dark shapes on the river. Two small building-shaped shadows. A few glimmers of light blinking from cracks of those standing structures—perhaps from gaslights between wooden planks in huts.

Dimming their headlights to pin pricks, they set down their small bags. Kirk pulled out the equipment and Surya quickly assembled the device. He watched her quick, sure hands, putting together pieces of plastic and the small computer card.

"Ready. Three, two, one," she said, and sprinted out into the darkness.

His satellite phone was ready, hooked up to a small device that would pair the signal to the one Surya had. His gaze followed her shadow as she moved, zigzagging in and out of trees and shrubs. Aiming his phone toward the sky, he called Dec's number, then punched in the codes.

He watched as she squatted close to the river bank. She had to secure the device somewhere in the open, away from trees. In the semi-darkness of that clearing, she had to be careful not to step on anything—traps, rocks, anything that could bring attention to her.

She stood up. He pressed the 'On' button to pair the signals. A red light, a few blinks, then green. Success.

She turned, heading back toward them.

That was when all hell broke loose.

* * * *

The crack of gunfire was sudden. Surya instantly dove to one side, rolling to the nearest shrub. She'd been extra careful, was sure she hadn't been seen. Besides, the shot didn't hit anything around her. She quickly took a look between two small branches.

There were shadows running toward her. Lights flared up and

shouts were heard, as if someone had been caught by surprise over at the enclosures and was giving a warning to others. She caught a few words. Filipino. The Abu Sayyaf terrorists were Filipino-based. She frowned. Weren't the rogue SEALs in league with them? So, if these weren't the guys they'd been following, who were these new intruders who had invaded the SEALs little hideout? And if they were intruders, what the hell was going on?

She studied the shadows scrambling toward her. There were three. The two in front were close together. The one behind appeared to be giving them orders. As they ran closer, she made out the words.

"Get in the boat. If you value your life, hurry up and get in the boat! My guys can only cover us for so long before everyone comes running out."

Surya blinked in reaction. That sounded like the man they'd talked to in the market earlier, the one she'd said was the rogue SEAL. Wait a minute, who was he running off with? She could come up with an answer, but there was only one way to find out. She couldn't let that boat get away.

* * * *

When the first shot rang out, Kirk's first reaction was to run toward Surya. Gasi stopped him, pointing at the lights flaring up in the semi-darkness. The gaslights gave shape to the liquid shadows and the outlines were now clear—two hut-like structures. He could see silhouettes coming out of doors, running. There were shouts of confusion. More shots rang out, some from his side of the clearing and others from the direction of the lights.

Kirk frowned. He and Gasi weren't firing any weapons. Who was over on this side?

Then he caught sight of the three figures rushing toward the shape on the river, the one he'd recognized as a boat of some kind. One of them stumbled and was dragged up by the one behind, who was yelling at them.

"He got them in. Go, go, go!" someone about a dozen meters

away from where he and Gasi were hidden shouted, startling Kirk into ducking behind a tree for protection. Then he saw more figures emerging from the nearby clumps of bushes. He made a quick count. Three. They'd been there all along. His heart went to his throat at the thought of Surya creeping around the shadows only minutes ago. Had they seen her?

He turned his attention back to the most important thing—Surya—and his whole being came to a stop when he realized her intention. She was running toward the boat. What the fuck was she doing? There were shots everywhere. The three men heading toward the boat would shoot her before she could—

Another group of men were rushing from the lit area, shouting obscenities. And, in the midst of the chaos, other dark shapes suddenly popped up out of nowhere from the direction of the river. A familiar war cry rose in the air.

"Hooooo-Yahhhhhh!"

Kirk rushed out of his hiding place. If the first one was hell breaking loose, this one was definitely a bigger, noisier one just arriving.

"Gasi, those are my guys showing up for the party. You stay put!" he yelled as he started off.

He saw Surya leaping like some pirate into the boat.

"No!" he shouted. "Surya!"

Dammit. She was going to go off without him again. From the corner of his eye, he caught movement and ducked just in time as a shadowy figure came at him with something long, knocking the small gun he was holding out of his hand. As he rolled back to his feet, his low headlight caught the attacker's face. One of the men from the market. He came at Kirk again with his weapon, a curvy blade on a long handle, a remade machete, perhaps, for cutting down higher branches.

Kirk knew the longer weapon had a better reach, so he dove to the left, rolling several times, as he groped for his weapon belt. The flash of the long blade slashed the air and hit the branch of the shrub next to him. Snatching up the broken branch with one hand, he turned to use it to stave off the next assault while his other freed his spare weapon from the holster.

Suddenly his opponent let out a howl of pain and turned in another direction. Kirk's dim light caught a smaller figure standing behind the man. It was Gasi, waving his stick. He had obviously used it hard enough to get the enemy's attention.

The man towered over Gasi's smaller stature, but that didn't seem to bother him at all. He countered each slash with his own stick and seemed to be using both ends of it as he bashed the bigger man on the knee, then turned and jabbed with the other end, causing another growl of pain.

Kirk couldn't wait to see the outcome of the fight. Gasi appeared to be able to handle it. He had to get to the moving boat.

He made a run for the river again, ignoring the gunfight going on. The shouts mostly came from the men rushing from the huts. They were carrying lanterns and the area became brighter as light appeared here and there. He could see the boat Surya had jumped into. The engine rumbled as it moved slowly at first, going around a dark bobbing object in the water. He suddenly realized it was what the SEALs called a "rubber ducky," their CRRC—Combat Rubber Recon Craft—used precisely for missions like this. He caught sight of another similar silhouette not far ahead. Two of them. Good, but did they know what was happening? He sure as hell wasn't sure.

Besides the initial war cry, the SEALs who had arrived were not as vocal as the enemy, instead letting their weapons do the talking. They easily took out the first ones carrying the lanterns. While the shooters stayed in position, others scrambled up the river bank. There was just enough light to catch running figures in muddy camo engaging in hand-to-hand combat with those who had run down the embankment. It was clear they were caught by surprise at the number of intruders in their territory because Kirk kept hearing shouts of *"Kiri! Kiri! Disitu! Pusing kanan!"* He recognized those words from his short lessons with Surya in the car—left, left, over there, turn right. Clearly, the overwhelmed kidnappers were confused about where to turn.

He didn't want to get caught up by friendly fire. When he ran close enough, he whistled and sharply called out, "Hawk! It's me,

Kirk Ryan!"

A figure turned. "Get your ass over here."

He did so. Explanation had to be quick. "The Americans we're after are behind us and are coming down here. No idea what's going on, but the rogue SEAL has taken off with the two prisoners. I have a feeling they're trying to figure out who you are and what's happening."

Hawk didn't turn to look at him, his focus on shooting down the easy targets holding the lanterns. "How many?" he asked.

"Can't tell. One tried to get me alive, obviously to ask questions, but my guide is fighting him. There were two men with the SEAL earlier today, so at least two I know of. I need to go after the boat that just took off, Hawk. Surya's on it. So are the prisoners."

"Cucumber!" Hawk barked out.

"Aye, Sir!"

"Take Ryan on the rubber ducky and chase that fucking SEAL on the boat." Hawk finally turned. His voice was calm as he headed off toward the woods with his weapon. "Put on the spare helmet to talk to Declan. Jazz, you're leading the raid. Zo, you and I are going hunting back there."

"Aye, Sir!"

"Copy!"

"My guide—Gasi—is the very short one. You can't miss him," Kirk added as he donned Hawk's helmet.

A tall, dark shape loomed near him. That must be the coxswain, the one in charge of the boat.

"Follow me," the man said.

"Cucumber?" Kirk asked, recognizing the fellow. "Umm...Lucas?"

Cucumber was a strange moniker for a SEAL to have. The man's teeth were very white in the moonlight.

"Let's go for a boat ride, young man. Hope you don't get too seasick."

* * * *

"I knew you weren't just a friend to a bunch of thieves. I don't recognize you, so you can't be working for MacKenzie. You're part of the American negotiating team, aren't you?"

Surya nodded. "And you're the kidnapper." She glanced at the two people lying face down on the boat, with the man's weapon pointed at them. "But why are Americans kidnapping our people and using Abu Sayyeh terrorists to front them? That's the confusing part."

The man laughed bitterly. "Yeah, that's the million dollar question. You shouldn't be here. Now you're probably going to die."

Surya cocked her head. "Probably?"

The boat was slowly picking up speed after navigating past several other dark shapes. From the sounds of combat behind them, she guessed they belonged to the SEAL team Kirk had been telling her about.

Kirk.

She pushed her worry for him firmly out of her mind. He was all right back there. He wouldn't come running after her when there was a firefight happening.

"It all depends on how good you negotiate."

"You got a name? Hard to negotiate without names. Mine's Surya."

"Mark. These two here are your scientists. It took me two days to figure out where those two-faced fuckers had hidden them. Now, what I want to know is, if you aren't with MacKenzie, who are those fucking SEALs who suddenly appeared out of nowhere? I can recognize a CRRC sitting on the river even if I were blindfolded."

"Must be because you're a SEAL too, right? From that tattoo?" Surya asked. She slowly took a step closer. "So, you took the prisoners from the terrorists. What's up with that? I thought you and they were buddies."

Mark waved his weapon and pointed it to the right. "That's close enough. You can sit down right there." He angled his face toward the front of the boat. "How much further to the island, Jackson?"

"Fifteen to twenty minutes, depending on conditions."

"Good. We'll meet the rocket deadline."

Surya frowned. "Island? You're heading to where they have the rocket? But isn't that defeating your purpose then?"

She couldn't quite make out his expression in the dim light given off from the engine room, but there was a strange stillness to Mark's stance. He gestured to her to sit down again and she obeyed.

"Will the good scientists please get up and go into the cabin?" Mark continued. "If things go well, you won't get hurt and will be back in the States in no time. Come on. The doorway to your left. Just go down and wait. Don't come up for any reason because if bullets start flying, you might get shot."

The two scientists got up slowly and complied with Mark's orders. Surya leaned back against the seat. She still had her weapons in her belt, although her chances of shooting an armed SEAL before he got her were absolutely nil.

"You do know there will be other SEALs on that island, right? Probably this MacKenzie about whom you're so concerned," she said.

"I'm counting on it," Mark said very quietly. "Oh, listen to that. Your friends are behind us."

* * * *

The CRRC was a vehicle for recon work. It offered no protection; there was no hiding from the enemy in open waters. The boat ahead moved steadily but not too quickly, as it navigated toward the deeper waters.

"He can hear us, so keep low," Lucas said. "He isn't shooting at us, though. Either he's in a hurry or he doesn't care. Or maybe the asshole doesn't want to make more SEALs angrier at him."

Kirk nodded. He'd been relating what had happened to Declan via the helmet mic and Lucas had been listening in. They'd concluded the men at the market had been looking for the forbidden territory to retrieve the prisoners. Why the terrorists had kept the location a secret from their "friends" hadn't been sorted out yet. However, it was apparent their arrivals—his and then Hawk's team—had been right at the moment the Americans had freed the scientists and were heading to the boat they were currently on.

"Declan has updated your commanders that there are two groups. The confusion will be sorted out once the dust settles. Sorry you're missing the action, Lucas." He didn't think he should call the big guy Cucumber. "They're tracking Surya's GPS right now."

Lucas glanced at him. "That's the GEM operative, right?"

"Yeah."

He grinned. "She'll kick that fucker's ass."

In spite of his worry, Kirk grinned back. "Yeah."

"Kirk," Declan's voice interrupted.

"Right here, Declan," Kirk said.

"It looks like he's taking Surya and the scientists to where Jed and my team are stationed."

Kirk sat up in surprise, then hunched back down. "What? He's heading toward your operation?"

"Jed traced the sale of the rocket and we've tracked it to here. We've been pinpointing the exact location quietly, hoping to get the terrorists before or while you're negotiating, but it looks like we're ditching that plan."

"No kidding." What the hell was that rogue SEAL up to?

"You're probably ten minutes away."

"He just killed the engine, Sir." Lucas interrupted the mic exchange. "I did too."

"Follow closely." Hawk's voice came on. He must have been listening in too, while coordinating his combat operation back in the jungle. "He's trying to keep his presence quiet. That means he won't shoot at you. Declan, you there?"

"Yes, over."

"Boy's on a solo mission. Apparently, he left behind the mercenaries he'd hired and they're plenty mad here. He has an agenda."

"So what do you think he's up to?" Kirk asked.

"The mercs don't know but they told me there are two SEALs on that boat. Two dishonorable traitors who betrayed our code. They know it and right now, they know their asses are history. Declan, what do you think?"

"Desperate men and desperate measures," Declan said. "Kirk, whatever they're planning, it's likely going to turn bloody. Get your weapons ready. Cucumber, much as I'd rather do it myself, shoot to kill."

"Copy, Sir," Lucas said.

Kirk readied his weapons as Lucas paddled the watercraft closer to the boat. The SEAL controlled the movement with ease, causing hardly a ripple as his oar cut through the dark waters.

"Why do they call you Cucumber?" Kirk asked, his curiosity getting the better of him. "I know they give out the nicknames to suit the personality. For you, I'd assume something with 'Big' in it, like 'Big Man'."

"It's for my big dick," Lucas told him in a matter-of-fact voice, as if it was quite a normal reply.

Kirk sighed. Fucking sailors. Why did he even think there would be any other answer but an anatomical reference?

"Forget I asked," he said.

There was a short silence as they waited. He wanted desperately to get on that boat to make sure Surya was safe. A desperate SEAL was a dangerous SEAL.

* * * *

The other SEAL came out.

"What's going to happen to her?" he asked. "When's Vadim arriving?"

"He isn't."

Surya watched as Mark silently moved from behind and smashed the butt of his weapon on the back of his friend's head. The other man crumpled to the ground. She didn't move as Mark efficiently tied him up. He then stood and came toward her.

"I know you have a tracker on you," Mark said, "so you're coming with me. Makes things easier when they know where I'm heading."

"Why did you do that to your buddy?"

He glanced back. "He has to live to tell our side of the story, I guess."

She didn't like the tone of his voice. "Being all mysterious will not save you," she told him. "If MacKenzie is on that island and you want to talk to him, just give up to the ones behind us. Isn't that the easiest way?"

Mark laughed. "Nothing's easy for the SEALs," he told her. "We're getting on this inflatable boat and heading to the island. Now, I know you're armed and thinking about using it on me, but can you hold off until we get on land? There will be fireworks enough then to lure your terrorists out to investigate. And if you're any good at it, I'll need you to start shooting at them for me."

"Why would I want to protect you?"

"Because I know where the rocket is. That's why MacKenzie and his team are on the island, right? To take out the missile. We're out of time. He'll be sending his men on this boat soon. They'll find your scientists safe and sound and my sleeping buddy will explain it all when he wakes up. Let's go."

Surya had to hand it to her captor. He was in full cocky SEAL mode and wasn't going to take no for an answer. Damn it. She hadn't even spent enough time vacationing to justify the expense of her hotel room and she was going to get killed by friendly fire. She'd been planning fun things to do with Kirk and food too.

* * * *

Kirk turned to Lucas. "Declan's sending Brady and a few others to the boat. Get ready to—"

"Movement," Lucas said. "Looks like our guys are leaving the boat on an inflatable."

"How many?" Kirk asked, leaning forward.

"Two figures."

"Just the SEALs? Where are the prisoners?"

"Not with them."

Kirk activated his mic and related what they saw to Declan.

"Brady's on his way," Declan told them, "I've informed him to be careful of explosives, just in case. We'll find out about the situation soon. Follow the inflatable, Cucumber."

"Aye, aye, Sir."

Kirk wanted to be the one going on the boat. Explosives. *Please let Surya be tied up and be safe.* He didn't want her moving around.

"Wait. Surya's GPS is beeping from the inflatable."

What? Surya was with the rogue SEAL? Kirk tapped on his mic.

"Why is he taking her and not one of the scientists?"

"I'm thinking he knows we'll be meeting him on the beach," Declan said.

Kirk tapped Lucas on the shoulder as he picked up the paddle. "I want to be on that beach before any firefight, Cucumber. I want to negotiate for my girl."

"We'll be there," Lucas assured him.

CHAPTER SIX

Surya let Mark pull her by the arm as she got out of the boat. He steadied her while she found her footing in the wet surf. She knew someone had been following them as Mark paddled toward the beach. He'd made no attempt to turn around to stop them. There were shadows on the dunes, waiting. He didn't seem to care he was surrounded either. She felt cold metal against her throat.

"Sorry. You have to play hostage a bit," Mark said. "Don't want them to start shooting yet. Damn SEALs. We're a trigger-happy lot."

"Thanks for using me as a shield," she told him dryly.

"I'm hoping it won't come to that. You're a sexy woman, by the way. Another time, another lifetime, ah…but I'm married. I love my wife and baby. Got distracted by that perfume of yours for a second there."

He was in remarkably good spirits for someone surrounded by people after his blood. "If you get me killed, you won't see them again, you know."

He was silent. "Just let me do the talking," he told her.

They started approaching the group as the other side moved toward them. They met up midway. She heard sounds from the arriving craft behind them too.

It was an eerily quiet moment. Steely-eyed men with weapons studying them with lethal gazes. There were three figures standing a few feet in front of the group. Surya didn't know who they were but she could tell they were in charge of the team behind them. The MacKenzies, perhaps?

"My judge and jury," Mark said. "I knew you would be here, Declan and Shane."

"If I'd known you were one of the traitors, I'd have killed you myself when you came to visit," one of the men said.

Surya could feel the leashed anger in the air. So she was right. Those two standing close to each other must be the MacKenzie brothers. Who was the third one over there?

"I know, Shane. Declan. I'm very sorry. About everything. About your mother."

"Fuck your apology! If you're man enough, let the woman go, come here and let me show you how sorry I'm gonna make you.," the one on the left said.

Surya felt Mark pulling her tighter against him. "Can't do that, Shane. There's no time left, with the clock ticking. I can't go back with you. Look, you can shoot me here and end it but it's not going to stop that missile. I can."

"What are you saying?" Declan spoke up.

"Someone's finger is on the button. The moment they see a whole team of commandos storming them, the missile goes off toward Bali, wrong time or not. The negotiation meeting you guys set up wasn't going to stop it. They just wanted the money in their account—then everyone would die and they'd get the notoriety. The only way to stop them is if I go in alone. I've sent a message saying I'm coming in with Vadim's money for the hostages. That's Petrovich's second. He's the one in charge now." Mark turned to Shane. "I'm glad you killed the son-of-a-bitch. Your mother—"

"You aren't fit to say anything about my mother," Shane said, his voice low and furious. "Dec, don't listen to him. Just fucking put him down so we can go locate the rest of these terrorists."

"Let me fucking get them for you and then you can come get me afterwards," Mark said tensely.

"I'll—"

Declan put a restraining arm on his brother. He turned to the figure quietly standing beside him "Jed?"

Surya frowned. Jed? As in Number Nine? She'd never met the top commando of the outfit that had merged with hers, but had heard lots of stories. The man they called Ice Man. The one who finished the job. The one who was after those who had killed their fellow operatives in that incident five years ago which had resulted in the GEM/COS merger.

"We have the scientists. Brady rescued them and is standing guard over the second traitor from your circle. As I see it, I need to stop the missile without an international incident involving unsanctioned SEALs. Let him do his job." Unlike Shane's, Jed's voice was emotionless. Cold, even. "Where's Vadim, man? I'll take care of that loose end."

"No, Vadim is mine," snarled Dec.

"Fine. Vadim's yours. Give us the info."

Mark only hesitated a second. "Don't know who you are, but I'm giving Surya here a piece of paper with the last known location. Also, my cell phone for you to trace the calls. All I need is Dec and Shane to agree to one thing."

"You're in no fucking position to negotiate about anything, asshole," Shane said in a cutting voice.

"What?" Dec asked.

"I want you to promise to take care of my wife and kids. They're safe right now but not for long if Vadim and his people find out what I've done. They've threatened to kill our wives and kids."

"All you guys had to do was come to me. You made your choice," Shane said.

"And I'll pay for it. You think it was easy? God knows I've betrayed you and my friends. I can't betray my wife and kid, you understand? I need you to promise to take care of them, if not for me, for the sake of being a SEAL taking care of family. You have no idea, no idea at all, Shane. You're always been the player, always able to come and go as you please. You don't have a woman or care about someone so much that the idea of her being dead strikes fear in your soul every night you're out on a SEAL mission."

Shane's mouth opened, as if he was about to give another angry reply, then his lips pursed into a straight line. "Go," he finally said.

He turned away, adding, "And you're wrong about my not understanding. There is always another way."

Surya didn't want to, but she was beginning to feel sorry for Mark. Maybe he did make the wrong choice, betraying his SEAL brothers and country, but he'd been thinking about his own family's safety.

"You swear you'll take care of Shelly and my kid."

"I'll make sure they're safe," Declan said, quietly.

"And I'll make sure all the other families are given protection," Jed continued. "Now, I'm coming right behind you to make sure you do your job."

Mark pushed Surya forward, then turned around, with her still tucked in front of him. They walked backwards slowly, away from the group. He whispered in her ear, "Goodbye, Surya."

It was clear Mark Walters was intending to sacrifice himself tonight. In her world as a GEM operative, mingling with refugees and displaced 'fighters', she'd seen enough examples of men and women who had given up. There were some who just sat down and gave up. Others who became hardened about their lot in life and used their bitterness in bloodshed. Then there were those who had decided to make a last stance, sacrificing themselves for that one bit of victory.

She understood Mark's position, even perhaps more than he did. They all lived and breathed the covert lifestyle. Each sacrifice was acknowledged, and in times of war, sometimes celebrated. Because in something lost, there was also much gained.

She turned and kissed him softly on the cheek. "Goodbye, Mark. *I* forgive you. Now, shove me hard onto the sand so I can get their attention off you for a few seconds."

She felt the wetness of his cheek, as if he was crying. He pushed her hard and she yelped out loud as the others rushed forward to her. Someone pulled her to her feet. It was Kirk. She stumbled forward in surprise. He held her tighter.

"Babe, you can stop acting. I saw you kiss him goodbye."

She wrinkled her nose at him and turned to face the others. "He has on a vest. I think it's full of explosives."

"Get out of here, all of you," Jed ordered. "There will be enough uniforms out here soon and only my team has permission for this international venture. I'll call you, Dec, when this is over. Please get my scientist back safely to Hawk, as well as the operative who was with him, if he's still alive. Hawk knows who to contact."

"We do not sanction suicide missions, Jed. I'm going after Mark," Dec said.

Jed stepped in front of him. "No, we had this talk before. Nothing comes between me and saving the lives of those at the Interpol Convention. I'm giving you Vadim, who is responsible for all this. That SEAL over there? No longer your responsibility. He's not on any authorized mission. We clear?"

"Fuck you, McNeil." Declan said, his voice cold and deadly.

If he'd said that to Surya, she would have cocked her weapon and prepare to defend herself. It was the kind of voice that would scare the person to whom he was addressing.

But Jed just turned and started walking away. "Maybe later. You've plenty to keep you busy, Dec. Get off this island so I can do my job. Surya? T says you're wasting your vacation time." He didn't look back as he went off in Mark's direction.

The tension felt like an elastic band. These SEALs had a code about never leaving any of theirs behind, and now, they were going to do exactly that. Any moment now, Surya knew it could snap and someone was going to get hurt. This wasn't the place to go psychological. Time to use her skill to distract them.

"Well." She exhaled a sigh. "He sure knows how to chew up scenery."

"Did Mark Walters really give you a note and his cell phone?" Kirk asked.

She nodded. She'd felt him shove something into her side pocket. "Want it now, Mr. MacKenzie?"

"Yes. We'll all leave now and get farther out in the water."

"Then what?" Kirk asked.

"We wait to see if he succeeds in doing what he said he would do. McNeil's with him to make sure the job gets done, but we're all going to watch and then we'll sail into international waters."

Surya slipped out of Kirk's arms and started off. She wasn't going to just hand over the note and not get what she wanted.

"Where are you going?"

"I'm not going with you crazy kids," she said. "I have a dream vacay to finish. You can come with me to get that note for your boyfriends here or I can mail it, along with your stupid bags."

Kirk stared after her. "Surya!"

She started running toward the rubber boat. Maybe she'd have a whole pack of men coming after her. That would make Jade laugh, for sure. She knew her friend would understand. This whole operation was a favor for her anyway. She didn't have to follow any damn protocol.

Hell, she'd been hoping Kirk would follow. She really, really wanted to be with him this time. Mark's love for his wife made her ache with need. She wanted Kirk to get to know her so well that he'd love her like Mark loved his wife.

* * * *

Kirk took a few steps, then stopped himself. He couldn't just abandon—

"Just go, man," Dec dismissed him. "We all do what we have to do to get the job done. I suspect your handler will call and tell you not to bother negotiating. Get in touch with me ASAP. She'll hand over the note and cell phone once you're out of the dark. Shane, let's get to Brady and have a talk with Mark's partner. Jed's right. We've get out of here before the local authorities come and take him away from us."

Kirk didn't need to be told twice. He ran after his woman.

"Hell, his job includes a dream vacay?" he heard someone behind him grumble.

"GEM operative, dude. He won't be dreaming or vacationing much."

Kirk reached out and caught Surya's hand and she turned her face toward him. The moon shone right on her expression and it made him catch his breath. They both ran, side-by-side, toward the inflatable.

"Last one in gets a spanking later," she told him.

"*Perempuan jahat*," he retorted. "Your ass is mine."

* * * *

Mark turned to the man who had silently followed him. He'd kept up without any trouble, which told him, in spite of being a dozen or so years older, he was in top condition.

"This is it." Mark pointed to the barricaded compound. "I know how to get in and out of there."

"You lied, didn't you? They don't know you're coming."

He gave the other man credit. Not only in good shape, but had the brains to see through Mark's desperation. What was his name again? Jed. "The woman back there. She said something earlier. We take care of our friends, she said. That's where I've failed. I've let my friends down, men who had my back when I needed them, men who fought beside me for years. I didn't think it through and it's cost the life of Dec and Shane's mother. She was the sweetest lady, after my own mother." Mark looked away. "I'm ashamed. Yet, I'm also not. I've bought enough time to get my own wife and baby to safety. I've got your promise that they'll be taken care of. Right?"

"Yes."

He nodded. "I have to believe you. They're no longer my friends, my teammates, my blood brothers, yet Surya's words gave me hope. Because friends take care of each other, she said. Even though you and I aren't, I have to take you at your word. This is how fucking wrong my world has become. I have to depend on strangers other than my own friends." He took in a deep breath and continued, "I've been inside there before and have made sure there are places for me to sneak back in. I'm a fucking SEAL. I don't trust any damn terrorist. I'm going in there and will take out the whole damn nest. I'll need half an hour. Goodbye, Sir."

The man gave him his hand. After a moment's hesitation, Mark shook it and discovered a card in his palm.

"The world isn't black and white, son," Jed said, his low gravelly voice soft in the semi-darkness. "If you survive this, if you get this job done, get ahold of me."

"And if I don't get it done?" Mark countered. It was highly unlikely he would make it out in time. He'd already accepted that fact. But this man's offer made him curious.

Jed cocked his head to the side. His strange light eyes gleamed in the moonlight. "I suppose a SEAL can't always beat the odds," he said. "Good luck."

Mark watched him disappear into the trees. Fucking weird fuck. What kind of man would throw out a challenge like that when there was no hope? He took a deep breath and turned toward the compound.

"Beat the odds," he muttered.

* * * *

Using binoculars, they all watched from afar. Waiting.

Then, there was a slow roar, an avalanche of sound that echoed like ominous thunder, the familiar rumble of explosives. The whole island lit up, flames shooting miles high in the distance.

Soon, there would be helicopters and air patrols on the way. McNeil had a way of getting governments to cooperate, especially when the glory became theirs to take. Saving a convention full of Interpol personal—that would make worldwide headlines. The SEALs faded into the darkness, their CRRCs taking them back to the waiting submarine. The other operatives guided their crafts into international waters to await further orders.

Dec and Shane grimly looked on for a second or two longer. Then they too turned.

"Home," Dec said.

"Then we go after the bastards, one by one," Shane said.

* * * *

Dear Reader,

There is an EPILOGUE and notes of interest from my research after this page. The epilogue shows the connection of MacKenzie Securities' scientific research with my Super Soldier Spy project's experimentation with exoskeleton and brainwave machines (Jed's and Helen's series). It was awesome to be able to work my spy themes into Liliana's world and vice-versa.

I hope you enjoyed this story. If you did, perhaps you would like to share it as a review so other readers will find this book too. It is so important to have a written review (not just rate it) because they are what counts for the author, not only as feedback, but also as the way to get promotions and ads. This is because some companies do not bother with books which have fewer than 30 reviews.

Thank you so much! You know all my furbabies and I appreciate your taking the time!

Regards,
Gennita

You can read Jed's story in VIRTUALLY HERS
You can read Hawk's story in HUNTER
You can read Jazz's story in PROTECTOR
You can find out about Cucumber's cucumber in WARRIOR

Sign up for newsletters: Jenn@Gennita-Low.com

EPILOGUE

Encrypted message from Uncle JD

Dec, regarding the agreed upon exchange of information. Your science notes were very helpful. Here's what's in the works at DARPA. Read memo and special attached notes. Make your own conclusions.

Regards,
Uncle J

MEMO
FYEO (For Your Eyes Only)

Cc: Intelligence Security Command (INSCOM), Los Alamos Task Force Unit Chief Scientist for Operation <redacted>; Armed Forces Medical Intelligence Center (AFMIC) Task Force Unit Chief Bio-Scientist for Operation Bio-Bot; Defense Intelligence Agency (DIA) Asymmetrical Strategic Counterintelligence Warfare Task Force Unit Chief for Operation <redacted>; Comptroller of Special Activities, General Accounting Office (GAO); COS COMMAND <redacted>

Past memo collected from various sources regarding human

augmentation.

Re: The Virus Program

Unclassified 2003 DARPA (Defense Advanced Research Projects Agency) Report: "The human is becoming the weakest link. Sustaining and augmenting human performance will have significant impact on Defense missions and systems." (http://www.ratical.org/ratville/CAH/superSoldier.pdf)

Latest DARPA budget request to fulfill projects researching on:

* cracking the brain's neural codes

* manipulating complicated machinery or remote-controlled weapons by thought alone (robotics and thought manipulation divisions) (Re: MACAQUE EXPERIMENT—success in manipulation of robotic arm with implanted brain sensors in monkeys)

* more work on the exoskeletons for Human Performance Augmentation. The $40 million program is already midway through the projected six-year run, experimenting on amplification of human muscle movements through a super body suit for the average soldier.

DARPA plans for further augmentation marrying brain and muscle power are challenged by the natural boundaries of human endurance.

On the $20 million Continuous Assisted Performance program, DARPA Director Tony Tether in a statement to the House Government Reform Committee: "The CAP is investigating ways to prevent fatigue and enable soldiers to stay awake, alert, and effective for up to seven consecutive days without suffering any deleterious mental or physical effects and without using any of the current generation of stimulants."

DARPA's top-secret still classified bio-research and human augmentation programs are also up for more funding. Identities of all operatives in program to be held top secret.

Dr. Paul Saffo, research director at the Institute for the Future in Menlo Park, Calif., from interview, please click on link to hear entire quotation:

"Human augmentation is coming; the only question is how soon. This stuff is being worked on in all sorts of places all over the world.

I'll give you three options. We can stay in it and be state of the art and deal with the moral issues. We can get out of it completely and be bystanders. Or we can do this half-assed thing in the middle. Now, of those three options, which one do you think is rational?"

Of interest to Dr. Kirkland pertaining to his questions on remote viewing: Military Applications of Post-Quantum Physics: http://www.qedcorp.com/Q/ChiaoBell.html.

NOTES OF INTEREST

1. There was an Interpol Convention held in Bali on Nov. 7, 2016. It was the 85th Interpol General Assembly, attended by representatives from 167 countries.

2. Also in the news around that time was the kidnapping of several foreigners by Aby Sayyeh terrorists. I used both pieces of news to form my own story.

3. DARPA

The Defense Advanced Research Projects Agency is an agency of the U.S. Department of Defense responsible for the development of emerging technologies

Of all the acronyms and agencies above, only DARPA is real. It is run by the Department of Defense. DARPA works on many, many cutting-edge technologies for the Defense Department and through the years, have also used their work to advance science for the betterment of life. Their research in the use of exoskeleton skin for injured veterans is one of these exciting projects.

While coming across many versions of projects called Super Soldier in my research, it occurred to me (while on the rooftop!) that it would be fun to write about a Super Solder SPY. A Female Super Soldier Spy. And thus started my deep research into the world of virtual reality, exoskeleton skin, remote-viewing and government secret programs. I had fun creating my own Super Soldier Spy in Helen Roston, a GEM operative, in my SSS series (Virtually Hers). All the projects are based on real government experiments that have been or are being conducted on humans and robots.

4. CRRC (Combat Rubber Recon Craft)

This is a specially fabricated rubber inflatable boat often used by United States Navy SEALs and Marines. It is used for inserting lightly armed night-raiding parties. They can be dropped out of a helicopter or launched from a ship and even a submarine.

DISCOVER THE LILIANA HART MACKENZIE FAMILY COLLECTION

Spies & Stilettos by Liliana Hart
Trouble Maker by Liliana Hart
Rush by Robin Covington
Never Surrender by Kaylea Cross
Avenged by Jay Crownover
Bullet Proof by Avery Flynn
Delta: Rescue by Cristin Harber
Hot Witness by Lynn Raye Harris
Deep Trouble by Kimberly Kincaid
Wicked Hot by Gennita Low
Desire & Ice by Christopher Rice

DISCOVER THE WORLD OF 1001 DARK NIGHTS

Collection One

Collection Two

Collection Three

Collection Four

Bundles

Discovery Authors

Blue Box Specials

Rising Storm

Liliana Hart's MacKenzie Family

ABOUT GENNITA LOW

Gennita Low writes sexy military and techno spy-fi romance. She also co-owns a roof construction business and knows 600 ways to kill with roofing tools as well as yell at her workers in five languages. A three-time Golden Heart finalist, her first book, Into Danger, about a SEAL out-of-water, won the Romantic Times Reviewers Choice Award for Best Romantic Intrigue. Besides her love for SEALs, she works with an Airborne Ranger who taught her all about mental toughness and physical endurance. Gennita lives in Florida with her mutant poms and one chubby squirrel.

To learn more about Gennita, visit www.Gennita-Low.com, www.rooferauthor.blogspot.com and www.facebook.com/gennita

DANGEROUSLY HOT

Hot Spies Series Book1
By Gennita Low
Now Available
Go to http://www.gennita-low.com/site/index.php for more
information

Kissing her turns up the heat to Dangerously Hot!

While working undercover looking for his missing brother, Luke meets the mysterious Nina who appears to know more than she's saying. Can Luke charm the sexy and dangerous Nina into assisting him?

Can they form the hottest partnership this side of Eastern Europe?

* * * *

CHAPTER ONE

Outskirts of Talinn, Estonia

The man was delicious to look at. What Americans would call "hot." Tall. Dark-haired and rakish-looking with that stubble. And, as always, that heated look in his jewel-green eyes gave her a sudden need for a long cool drink, preferably with vodka.

She was long past the point of wondering why he affected her this way. He just did. At each meeting, she anticipated his gaze, so direct, so damn intimate, and each time, she couldn't help herself. She winked at him. And then, depending on the situation, they would pick up or exchange items in the middle of the place or one of them would back away, following the unspoken protocol of a first-come-first-serve basis.

It was part of the game. She could play it a bit hotter but knew she couldn't afford it. It was just too bad they were on opposite sides because she had a feeling it'd be more than a bit hotter.

Scorching, more like.

Her superiors wouldn't approve any consorting without their say-so. After all, she was their fixer. She couldn't be seen being friendly with someone who could use it against her.

But damn, he was hot. She waited for him to step back, do his usual two finger salute to acknowledge that she'd arrived first this time, but instead, he started walking slowly toward her.

She frowned. This wasn't their pattern. Nowadays, their respective agencies had agreed to do things with the least casualties as possible. Yes, some treaties actually included secret clauses like "first-come-first-serve," "positional operative compromise" and "negotiable exchange."

So civilized.

She didn't back away as he approached. Curiosity stopped her. He had a hand in his jacket, probably a weapon. It occurred to her she might be a target but she didn't think so. If he'd wanted to kill her, he'd have done so already from five meters away. Or any number of times she'd bumped into him the last ten or so months.

They'd never spoken to each other directly. He'd never touched her. Their long looks at each other had been when there were no witnesses.

She watched, unable to move, as his hands came up and cupped her face. Tilted it up. His thumbs rubbed her cheeks. She didn't do a thing as his head swooped down and his lips caught hers. His tongue swept into her surprised mouth. Tangled. Tasted. Vodka and lime. Five seconds, tops.

He stepped back and gazed down at her, those eyes cool and unreadable. The corners of his lips lifted slightly, a smile of a man who had just discovered a secret.

"I've wanted to do that for a while now," he softly said, that husky American Southern twang sending a tingle down her spine.

That voice was distinct, instantly recognized in the European underground. The Cowboy had a reputation of getting things done his way. But she had a reputation too, a lethal one.

She continued watching him as he disappeared into the shadows. Five seconds could get a man killed. Five seconds could change one's life.

* * * *

"So, did you make your move?"

Luke unzipped his leather jacket, shrugged out of it, and hung it on the hook by the entrance. His friend, Konstantin, continued regarding him from the small dining table as he walked to the fridge. Perusing his options, he closed it, and went for hard liquor instead. He went to sit across from his flat mate. He took a swig from the bottle.

Konstantin flapped the newspapers, folding it over, his dark eyes mocking him with a knowing gaze. "Was she that good? Or that bad?"

Ignoring Konstantin was pointless. He'd just continue riding him all night.

"Maybe I didn't see her," Luke said.

"And maybe cows don't fly. You have the lovesick look about you, buddy."

Luke grinned. Konstantin's trademark of over-the-top exaggeration was just what he needed to loosen the tension inside him. His frustration must really be showing. Konstantin had that "I got you pegged" look in his eyes. "Pigs. It should be 'and maybe pigs fly.' Cows already don't fly, Kostya."

"*Whatever.*" Konstantin copied the popular American slang term with bored perfection. He flicked his hand expressively. "You're changing the subject. You can't distract me from my quest."

His flat mate also loved online role-playing games. His current obsession was some medieval quest for magical weapons that pitted worldwide players against each other. Luke had watched him at his gaming sessions now and then, although it was beyond him why anyone, let alone someone who was in their business, would play a multi-level dungeon and dragons game for months on end without getting bored.

When asked, Konstantin had just shrugged and replied that it kept him on his toes, and besides, he met interesting people, from professors of medieval history to young men bored with their current factory jobs. Luke supposed those types were interesting to his friend only because they were ordinary people living safe, ordinary lives. He was so into it, he'd brought his current gaming character, Sir Constantinus, into his real-life dialogue, both amusing and somewhat disconcerting to some.

Luke took another swig and peered over the bottle. "And your quest is?"

"Come on, we all deal with information. Do you know how much I could get for proof that The Cowboy and La Niina are sitting on a branch?"

"In a tree," Luke corrected and frowned. "I should've known you'd try to sell information like that."

Konstantin snorted. "You don't care if I do or I don't. The ladies think The Cowboy is a handsome challenge anyway."

Luke hadn't chosen that nickname. They called him that because he was so obviously American, with his South Georgia drawl and his boots. It was a pretty useful one since it didn't sound particularly threatening and was easily identifiable. It didn't take too long for many in the underground network to get to know the name and it was the first one on their minds any time they needed something fixed that needed an American handler.

Exactly what he wanted. Information from the fringe. Non-network news.

As for La Niina, the woman given that handle of the cold front that swept through the oceans, was neither a child or frigid. In fact, she was all woman and smoldering hot.

ON BEHALF OF 1001 DARK NIGHTS,

Liz Berry and M.J. Rose would like to thank ~

Liliana Hart
Scott Silverii
Steve Berry
Doug Scofield
Kim Guidroz
Jillian Stein
InkSlinger PR
Asha Hossain
Fedora Chen
Kasi Alexander
Pamela Jamison
Chris Graham
Jessica Johns
Dylan Stockton
and Simon Lipskar

Printed in Great Britain
by Amazon

86559408R00062